Closed Horizon

PETER LANTOS is a Fellow of the Academy of Medical Sciences and in his previous life he was an internationally known clinical neuroscientist who has now retired from a Chair at the Institute of Psychiatry, King's College London. He is the author of numerous medical and scientific texts.

His previous book *Parallel Lines,* published by Arcadia, is the story of a boyhood journey from a sleepy provincial town in Hungary during the Second World War to the concentration camp in Bergen-Belsen. He has been living in London for more than four decades and *Closed Horizon* is his first novel.

PETER LANTOS

Closed Horizon

ARCADIA BOOKS

Arcadia Books Ltd

www.arcadiabooks.co.uk

First published in Great Britain by Arcadia Books 2012

A catalogue record for this book is available from the British Library.

ISBN 978-1-906413-97-2

Typeset in Minion by MacGuru Ltd
Printed and bound in the United Kingdom by
CPI Group (UK) Ltd, Croydon, CR0 4YY

Arcadia Books supports English PEN, the fellowship of writers who work together to promote literature and its understanding. English PEN upholds writers' freedoms in Britain and around the world, challenging political and cultural limits on free expression. To find out more, visit www.englishpen.org or contact
English PEN, Free Word Centre, 60 Farringdon Road, London EC1R 3GA

Arcadia Books distributors are as follows:

in the UK and elsewhere in Europe:
Macmillan
Brunel Road
Houndmills
Basingstoke
Hants RG21 6XS

in the USA and Canada:
Dufour Editions
PO Box 7
Chester Springs
PA, 19425

in Australia/New Zealand:
The GHR Press
PO Box 7109
McMahons Point
Sydney 2060

in South Africa:
Jacana Media (Pty) Ltd
PO Box 291784
Melville 2109
Johannesburg

1

Proclamation Day, Monday 22 October 2040, for the Republic of Great Britain, dawned with a downpour of biblical proportions. The storm was as violent as it was unexpected. Having a tropical storm in October was further evidence, the commentators later stated, that despite draconian legislation to reduce the pollution of the atmosphere, the planet was heading for environmental disaster. Older people with long memories recalled an October night in 1987 when an unexpected storm, created by ferociously strong winds reaching hurricane force in places, struck sleeping London and a large swathe of south-east England with devastating effect, leaving many dead people and millions of uprooted trees in its wake. Then as now, the Met Office failed to issue a warning.

Only superstitious people with the benefit of hindsight had claimed afterwards that the freak storm was a harbinger of the drama played out a few hours later in the Olympic Stadium, completely refurbished for the occasion.

The newly elected President was ten minutes into his speech. It was a brilliant oration: a firework display of phrases unburdened by any original thought; a roll call of well-rehearsed clichés. Oft-repeated justification for abolishing the monarchy. The anachronism of the old system. The case for the disestablishment of the Church of England. The threat of religious extremism. The never-ending terrorist menace. The poison of religion; of all religions. The inequality of the old system. The necessity of state control while maintaining individual rights. Comprehensive state education. Rewards in all walks of life according to achievements. Reinforcing the armed services. The promise of a bright future. One nation, one goal.

In his glass observation room, suspended high above and invisible to the crowd, the officer from Home Security responsible for the smooth running of the ceremony gradually relaxed as the speech neared its conclusion. None of his agents, carefully dispersed in strategic positions throughout, reported the slightest signs that might have indicated any disturbance or even a medical emergency. With his visor he scanned the stadium and then zoomed onto the presidential box until individual VIPs came sharply into focus. On the presidential face he could even study the remnants of a small spot which impatient presidential fingers had prematurely tried to remove, leaving behind an untidy bloody crust.

Suddenly, on an impulse that he could not explain even later, as his visor wandered to survey the crowd at random, he singled out a middle-aged woman sitting a few yards from the presidential box. She opened her handbag and delved into it with her right hand. A second later she withdrew her hand now covered with a thin silk scarf. From her seat she had an excellent view of the presidential box. For a split second the officer held the visor glued to the face of the woman, as if paralysed, recording every little detail: short-cropped auburn hair, no make-up, brown eyes, two-piece rust-coloured suit with a cream silk shirt beneath. No wedding ring on her left hand and the only jewellery she was wearing was a pearl necklace that looked both simple and expensive. A professional woman in her mid-forties, he thought, but even before completing his surveillance he realised he could wait no longer. The woman lifted her arm. The silk scarf slid down to reveal a gun.

At that moment the President ended his speech, and his last words were drowned in thunderous applause. For a second the officer was stunned by the noise coming through the open panel of his observation pod, reverberating and amplified. Then he picked up the gun and steadied his arm. Through the visor, the head of the unknown woman swam sharply into focus. As she was turning towards the presidential box, he drew a deep breath and targeted her left temple.

Those who were sitting around her suddenly realised what was happening. The officer saw the frozen fear and disbelief on their faces.

I cannot fail, he thought. To ease the final hurdle, he said aloud: 'I cannot fail.'

And then he pulled the trigger.

2

His naked body was drenched in sweat and his pillowcase was damp. He raised his head, using this movement to prevent himself from sinking back into the nightmare. The bedroom was still and silent: only the two ill-fitting shutters allowed a shaft of street light to seep through. In the darkness, he could sense rather than see Yasmina curled up next to him. She lay motionless, in a foetal position, deep in sleep, unaware of the impending dawn. Her even breathing reassured him. He looked at the old-fashioned alarm clock on the glass bedside table: it was half past four. Gently, so as not to disturb her, he pushed back the thick linen sheet and the woollen rug. Still shaken by the nightmare and unsteady on his feet, he made his way to the bathroom.

As he entered, all the lights came on: he had forgotten to override the automatic sensor by switching the control to night mode. For a few seconds he stood, blinded and paralysed. He sat on the edge of the bath for a while, the contact with the cool marble calming him down. He longed for a shower: the jet of cold water would finally release him from the grip of the night. He chose the large walk-in shower at the far end of the bathroom. Standing motionless under the cool stream of water coming from all directions, he finally resurfaced from the nightmare. The sprays stopped automatically as he stepped out and closed the heavy glass door of the shower behind him. He picked up one of the bath towels, rubbing and patting his body dry with the routine of an athlete. By now completely awake, he stood in the middle of the bathroom. Without looking at the mirror, he surveyed his body with detached objectiveness. He was not displeased by what he saw.

Mark Chadwick was thirty-two years old, and at 190 centimetres, taller than average with a well-proportioned body. Rowing in the summer, skiing in the winter and a weekly workout followed by a half hour swim kept him in good shape.

'Not bad for a doctor,' he used to say to fend off unsolicited comments in the gym. The mirror, framing his entire upper body to the point where the thin trickle of abdominal hair from the navel widens into the pubic tufts, reflected a smooth chest. He had black hair, one unruly lock falling over his forehead whenever he moved. This had annoyed him as a child, when he always opted for a short crop, and only at medical school had he allowed it to grow back. In recent years he had frequented an old-fashioned barber in Jermyn Street in whose shop he left a small fortune. Since Anne and now Yasmina both liked his hairstyle, it had hardly changed during the last decade.

He had inherited his mother's green eyes and long eyelashes. His lips, under a straight nose that betrayed a small scar, the result of a fracture suffered during a childhood brawl, had the plasticity of those whose friendly gestures are accompanied by a natural smile. Having finished this unscheduled night survey of his body, he returned to the bedroom.

After the brightness of the bathroom, it took a few seconds to adapt to the gloom. Gingerly, he climbed back into bed. Yasmina was still fast asleep, but her body had by now uncurled, and she was lying on her back with her right arm bent around her head, as if to frame it. The outline of her body was barely visible under the blanket. Looking at her he felt a sudden urge to make love but he dared not to move. At that moment Yasmina, still asleep, turned towards him, and Mark used this sudden intimacy to draw her close against his body. She opened her eyes and as he entered her, she wrapped her arms around his neck.

The alarm went off at exactly seven o'clock. When Mark finally awoke, the space next to him was empty. Yasmina had already gone. Only the rumpled sheets were witness of their lovemaking; the large woollen rug lay on the floor. Through the closed bathroom door he could hear running water. Mark got up and put on a dark blue towelling dressing gown. He walked to the windows to open the shutters: a ritual he cherished each morning.

The shutters had survived two centuries; even their flat, heavy metal bolts were original. This terraced house on the eastern side of Regent's Park was built by Nash in 1827 and many of its original features survived. Mark loved the house and counted himself fortunate to own it. Before their tragic deaths, his parents had lived in this house, and he envisaged that one day his children would grow up here. Unlike its more pretentious neighbours, this terrace was one of Nash's less bombastic designs, and what it lacked in grandeur was amply compensated for in the charm and the welcoming scale of its internal architecture.

He lifted the bolt from its holder and folded the shutter back into the architrave: first the left window away from the bed and then the right one, never the other way around. The beginning of the day was defined by never changing small rituals. Regent's Park lay in front of him in its autumn colours. The sun glinted on the cream stucco of the terraces, and he could survey the expanse of Cumberland Green and the trees beyond.

It was one of those exquisite October mornings when low-lying mist swims to cover the lawn and to swirl around tree trunks, before slowly lifting as the sun rises. Most of the trees still retained their leaves in the mild weather, but the first night frosts painted them yellow, rust and red. In the strip of sloping garden immediately in front of their house, the Japanese acer still had its full crown of deep purple leaves; few had been parched by the summer sun. A late blooming fuchsia still produced masses of crimson and deep purple blooms, its thinner branches bowed under the weight of flowers. The white geraniums in the antique lead planters by the iron railings also ignored the changing season, but the white lobelias planted amongst them had not survived.

The air was still. No one was around. Dew covered the

windscreens of the cars; it was too early for the neighbours to start their engines. Yet he could hear the distant whoosh of the commuters' cars on the Outer Circle, as they made their way from north London and the commuter belt beyond the M25 into central London and the City. Even in rain or under a grey sky, the view from his bedroom window never failed to lift his spirits. This early morning tranquillity formed a safe bridge between the night spent and the uncertainties of the coming day.

Mark and Yasmina's morning routine was a well-oiled affair. Although there was another bathroom on the floor above, they both used the one next to their bedroom. Since to prepare the breakfast was, by mutual agreement, Mark's task, he usually had first use of the bathroom. However, this morning was an exception and after Yasmina had finished her bath, Mark stepped back from the window and made his way to the bathroom. After another quick shower he dried himself, and from one of the built-in wardrobes in the adjoining dressing room he picked a lightweight grey suit with fine blue stripes and a light blue shirt. He selected a dark blue tie with a small white diamond pattern and put it into his briefcase; he would only tie it on arrival at the Institute.

From the master bedroom on the second floor, he walked down the elegant staircase: every step and the balustrade were original. As he entered the large drawing room on the first floor to collect some material for his seminar with his students later in the morning, he noticed that one of the two large sash windows of exquisite proportion that ran to the floor and opened onto a narrow balcony had been left open for the night. Yasmina again, he murmured, more with affection than irritation.

The kitchen, facing east, was flooded with the watery sunshine of autumn. The only blemish in the idyllic setting was nearby Albany Street – a road of fast, relentless traffic and a source of noise and pollution. Preparing breakfast for Yasmina did not take long: the menu was simple and barely changed during the week. Freshly squeezed orange or grapefruit juice, cereal and cups of freshly made coffee. He switched on Radio 3: the last movement of a Haydn symphony filled the kitchen. There was an unspoken agreement between him and Yasmina: they would not watch or listen to the news during their breakfast, preventing the intrusion of the outside world.

As Mark was putting the spoons on the glass table, he heard Yasmina's footsteps on the stairs. She was wearing a pair of tight-fitting, bleached jeans, emphasising her slim figure, a pale green polo neck sweater and dark blue suede moccasins. She looked stunning in the morning sunshine: a traditional Indian beauty, as many of Mark's friends commented with their eyes usually languishing on Yasmina's perfectly formed breasts.

Her dark brown hair, cut to a fashionable length barely touching her shoulders, framed an oval face that was dominated by brilliant brown eyes. With the exception of a pale lipstick applied more as a moisturiser than as additional colour to draw attention to her sensuous lips, she did not wear any make-up nor did she need to – her skin was luminous. She was tall for a woman but exactly in proportion to Mark: they were a perfect couple.

Over breakfast, as usual, they discussed the coming day. Yasmina had an early appointment at the British Library with one of her PhD students, Ted. The rest of the day was free for her research. Finishing her coffee, Yasmina stood up, and, bending over, kissed Mark tenderly on the top of his head, waved goodbye from the kitchen door and was gone.

For a couple of minutes Mark remained seated and watched, nearly motionless, as a ladybird climbed up the stalk of a geranium leaf in the box on the windowsill. It is time, he thought, to turn out these flowers damaged by early morning frost and replace them with mini-cyclamens, much loved by Yasmina.

He stood for a few moments, thinking about her. Mark had no doubt that it was her presence that animated their home. He knew that he owed a lot of his happiness at home – and success at work – to her support and understanding. The aura of her presence, like a strong perfume, permeated the entire house. Even after she left, an invisible imprint of her being lingered for a couple of minutes before the rooms became lifeless and closed down, waiting for her return. Without her the whole house was dead: a series of rooms which he could survey with the satisfaction of possession but without any emotional attachment, as if flicking through a glossy interior design magazine in the waiting room of his dentist in Upper Wimpole Street.

He stood up, cleared the table, checked the screen of the mini-portable and gave a sigh of relief. The registration number of his car, LS 39 VMR was flashing. His car was cleared to drive through central London to work. Mark, being a doctor, enjoyed priority, but despite this privilege, he had to confirm every morning whether, as a result of an increase in pollution or unforeseen emergency roadworks, private cars would be banned for the day from entering central London.

Cars did not have any particular attraction for him: they were neither status symbols nor phallic expressions of virility like some of the more esoteric sports cars now out of fashion, but mere vehicles of convenience to carry him from one place to another. Currently, he was the satisfied owner of a dark blue electric Volkswagen of last year's registration.

He was delighted with the news that he could drive, since the alternative would have taken much longer: a short brisk walk to Camden Town underground station to take the Northern Line to Elephant and Castle and then the rest of the journey on one of the buses to Camberwell Green. This morning he was particularly eager to get to work, for the new series of experiments scheduled to start today filled him with expectation. He might begin to see the fruits of many months of planning.

He picked up his car key from the hall table. His car, parked in the private driveway in front of the house, was waiting for him.

3

Driving south on the Outer Circle was a pleasure. The park had always captured him with its calming effect. He resented the way the Crown Estate had increasingly commercialised it by allowing and even encouraging international art fairs, food and wine tastings, and a variety of ethnic festivals in order to increase revenue. Yet it had remained an oasis of peace. A stroke of genius of town planning resulted in a green sanctuary in the middle of the metropolis, an illusion of Arcadia but with real wildlife. Whilst he and Yasmina were not avid birdwatchers, they counted more species in the trees of Regent's Park than in most of the countryside.

Only the proliferation of surveillance cameras intruded into the privacy of those who sought an escape from the noise and bustle of the city. Private cameras had been installed in the past but only during the last couple of years had they been planted not only on strategic points of the terraces bordering the park, but also on several buildings inside the park and, what annoyed Mark most, even on trees.

He passed the Royal College of Physicians on his left, a concrete edifice, so different from the surrounding Nash terraces and much maligned by those who had never set a foot inside. As he turned into Marylebone Road at St Andrew's Gate in Park Square East and, continuing down Euston Road, he was confronted by a forest of surveillance cameras. On specially erected columns and traffic lights, on rooftops and windowsills, on billboards and road signs, in gateways and underpasses, on flyovers and in school grounds, at bus stops and underground stations, at entrances to banks, shops, department stores and private

houses: they were omnipresent. They watched, scanned and followed everybody with their malevolent glass eyes, wherever one
was. Many more were hidden.

The more recent models, like those previously placed only at
important crossroads, stations, airports and public buildings,
but now more extensively installed to replace older cameras,
were equipped not only with voice recognition systems which
could record conversations, but also identified faces and patterns of behaviour. They had become part of everyday life. There
was no escape from them. For fun, Mark and Yasmina played
games: how many each could discover in a given area. One day
they counted 128 as they walked down from St Andrew's Gate to
the bottom of Gower Street, covering barely half a mile.

They were quite certain that, the cameras being so cleverly
camouflaged, they had overlooked a great many. In their nearest
underground station, Regent's Park on the Bakerloo Line, their
tally was thirty-one from street level down to the platform, an
amazing number considering that this stop, far from being a
busy hub, served only one line. Yet they should not have been
surprised: according to the Government's own statistics, a recent
survey confirmed the existence of thirty-five million cameras;
nearly one for every two British citizens.

This morning the traffic was quite fast, and Mark reached
Waterloo Bridge within ten minutes. The panorama from the
bridge, the highlight of the journey, was breathtaking and he
would have liked to stop but he knew that his licence would be
automatically endorsed. After reaching Camberwell Green, the
car slowed down over the final couple of hundred yards of gentle
rise before coming to a halt in front of the campus's underground car park.

The Institute of Cognitive Sciences rose eight floors over
Camberwell Road. The building was a good example of contemporary architecture with its simple but elegant lines, and judi-
cious use of glass and steel. It had been completed in 2038 and
officially opened by the King in the autumn of the same year:

one of the last public functions he performed before his abdication the next year following a national referendum. The marble plaque in the atrium, commemorating the event, would soon become one of the mementoes reminding people of the final chapter of more than a thousand years of monarchy.

For a long time the neighbourhood did not have a good reputation. Muggings and street fights were common. Small-time drug dealers had been supplanted by organised gangs, and turf wars had often ended in casualties. An innocent nurse was fatally wounded in a crossfire exchanged between two rival gangs one Christmas morning.

A temporary police station installed in the main building of King's College Hospital did not make much difference, and the police, finding the place too dangerous, soon withdrew. Nonetheless, a couple of months after the State of Emergency had been declared everything had changed. Even those who disapproved of the Government's non-compromising attitude to violence and terrorism reluctantly had to admit that the tough policies had worked. The drug dealers and muggers disappeared, and the streets were cleaned up. Within less than a year the neighbourhood had reverted to what it had not been for a long time: a peaceful south London district.

The electronic gate of the car park opened and a disjointed voice allocated him his parking space for the day: Dr Chadwick, Level two, number 243. He parked, switched the engine off, picked up his briefcase from the passenger seat and locked the car. As he was walking towards the lift, he recognised the voice of Nigel Ashworth, the chief physicist of the Department of Functional Neuroimaging, behind him.

'Good morning, Mark,' and as he caught up with him just in front of the lift door, he exclaimed: 'What awful news!' Since Mark looked uncomprehending, he explained: 'Someone tried to shoot the President yesterday at the Proclamation Ceremony. A mentally disturbed woman, apparently.' As Mark still did not respond, he added: 'She failed.' Neither Nigel's intonation nor his features betrayed whether he approved or disapproved of this sequence of events, since they both knew that the cameras around them were voice-sensitive and could pick up the quietest of murmurs. Slightly irritated by his colleague's lack of response, Nigel concluded, with the deflated air of someone whose news has failed to create a sensation: 'Then she was shot by one of the security men. You really didn't know?' And when Mark shook his head, he added: 'I can't believe you.'

'No, I didn't,' confirmed Mark with a sense of quiet satisfaction over the fact that on this occasion he had been protected from the outside world. A small but gratifying victory over the screens and cameras, the endless variety of information technology which like a malign and alien transplant had been growing beyond control, threatening to invade and overtake his own thoughts, to penetrate his life and finally to destroy the privacy of his very being. Suddenly he realised that during the last couple of years he had more and more come to agree with his grandfather with whom, when he was at school and later at university, he had had fierce arguments about the merits and dangers of information technology.

'No, we didn't watch television, surf on the internet or listen to the radio,' he said, 'we had a quiet evening at home, reading.' Mark wished he hadn't bumped into Nigel. Ashworth was one of the very few people at work whom he did not like; he found him intrusive and inconsiderate. To dislike a colleague pained him, yet in Ashworth's presence he could not bring himself to lower his guard. In conversations in the senior common room, Mark always felt the need to deflect Ashworth's direct questions, phrased with the expectation of an immediate and clear-cut answer, even when the subject would have required more thorough consideration.

The lift took them to their respective floors: Nigel left on the third, while Mark continued to the seventh, relieved to complete the journey on his own. His identity having been recognised by the sensor, the door of the department automatically opened and he entered the long straight corridor leading to his office.

His secretary was already at her desk.

'Good morning, Catherine. You're early today.'

'Good morning, Dr Chadwick. Did you have a nice weekend?'

Catherine had been working for him since the Institute opened and they had learned when exchanging early morning pleasantries on arrival, which questions needed a reply and which could be left hanging in the air.

Catherine was in her mid-fifties, a tall, stylish woman who preserved a youthful figure, and her impeccable choice of dress made her the most elegant employee in the department. When Mark saw her job application, immaculately set out in perfect English, he read with amazement that she specified her nationality as British-Welsh, hyphenated, just like that. Catherine was a self-confessed Welsh nationalist who harboured a deep-seated hatred of the National Government for aborting fuller autonomy of the principality, but these views she shared only with her boss and no one else.

Otherwise their relationship was restricted to professional matters with occasional forays into small talk about the weather, the varying standard of cooking in the Institute's canteen, about an evening at the theatre or at a concert. Their private lives were never mentioned, let alone discussed. In the etiquette of social contacts their exchanges took place within well-defined, yet unspoken boundaries that neither of them wished to trespass. This understanding was the source of a pleasant and relaxed ambience, a necessary lubricant to their daily interactions.

'Catherine, do you know what happened during the ceremony yesterday? Dr Ashworth was telling me that someone apparently attempted to shoot the President. Extraordinary!'

She did know and without prompting she gave a detailed account of the event. Finishing her report, she left no doubt that she was quite sorry that the President had escaped.

'Do they know who the woman was?' asked Mark.

'Her name hasn't been released. The police have to notify her family first but they haven't found the next of kin. She must have been a desperate woman. Didn't have much chance, did she?' Without waiting for an answer, Catherine turned back to her screen.

Occasionally, Mark wished that he knew more about Catherine. He felt certain that there were more remarkable facts about her life than having a retired, overweight husband and two daughters who were not particularly close to her. There must be a touch of rebellion beneath that cool façade, Mark thought, but if there was, Catherine had given no indication of any wayward thought, until her interpretation of the events in the Olympic Stadium.

His office was uncluttered and simply furnished. Facing north, the enormous plate-glass window yielded an astounding panorama of London, stretching from Chelsea Harbour in the west to Canary Warf in the east. For a minute he stopped to admire the view in front of him. Half of his desk was occupied by a bank of screens. The large collection of neuroscience textbooks made his office personal, distinguishing it from many others within the building.

The screens came alive as he keyed in his code. On the central monitor his daily schedule appeared, confirmed and signed off by Catherine.

09.00–10.00: Introductory tutorial for student volunteers in the Brain Bank.

10.00–12.00: Preliminary experiment in the Functional MRI Unit.

12.00–13.00: Seminar on the Future of Human Evolution by Professor Hugh Cameron, Cambridge University, in the Ground Floor Lecture Theatre.

13.00–14.00: Lunch with Professor Blakemore in his office to discuss the Health Sciences Research Council programme grant.

'The rest of the afternoon is free,' Catherine had added

reassuringly, knowing how much Mark treasured the second half of the day without appointments. Scanning the daily programme filled him with expectation. He looked forward to seeing his students: they were handpicked volunteers for a preliminary study, the brightest group for quite some time. If the first few screenings gave positive results, the door would open for submitting a major programme grant on thought reading to the Health Sciences Research Council for five years' support.

He looked at his watch, a vintage Patek Philippe he had inherited from his father. Its design was as simple as it was elegant: slim, sharply drawn black Roman numerals with slender black hands on a white face, encased in gold. Mark clearly remembered the moment his grandfather gave it to him on his sixteenth birthday, as a special present after Anthony had agreed that the older son should inherit the watch. His father was wearing it on the day he died: a painful reminder that the watch had somehow survived, but his father had not.

It was two minutes to nine. The Brain Bank was two doors down the corridor but instead of the panorama to the north, it afforded only the view of Camberwell's back streets facing south. Entering the room Mark could sense a feeling of anticipation: the twelve students, accompanied by Maria Lopes, the neuropsychologist, were already waiting for him.

They were third-year clinical students, selected from a much larger group, who had volunteered for the trial run. Six male and six female. Their CVs were scrutinised and their achievements, with exam results from the previous years, had been checked by their tutors. Their IQs had been assessed more than once and they had all been submitted by one of the best – in Mark's view the best – neuropsychologists one could find in London to the most comprehensive and vigorous psychometric testing.

Mark was fond of Maria Lopes and was delighted when she had agreed to collaborate with him on this project. She was a small Portuguese woman who could be easily overlooked, perhaps as a result of her stature or unassuming manner, until she started to give one of her brilliant assessments of her patients. Mark witnessed that on clinical grand rounds, attended by the most senior consultants, she often stole the limelight from some of her flashier colleagues.

Mark decided to start the tutorial with a brief description of the anatomy of the brain: to get over what might be dry for the students but was essential to an understanding of the fundamentals of the experiments. He switched on the projection system. A three-dimensional picture of the brain appeared on the large screen lowered from the ceiling. The image slowly rotated showing the main parts, starting with the top convexity, with the division between the two hemispheres, then the sloping sides and finally the flat base. Mark followed the projection with brief explanations of the most important structures as he glided along with the laser pointer and then, suddenly, he froze the image and zoomed to the front of the convexity of the cerebral hemispheres, enlarging a small area.

'As you know,' he said, pointing the slim laser beam to outline the frontal pole of the brain which suddenly turned red, 'this is the so-called pre-frontal cortex.' And then he proceeded to delineate the topography of this area, explaining the structure and function of its subdivisions, and its complex connections with other parts of the brain. He talked of neuronal circuitries; the types of nerve cells that form these structures and the various chemical molecules, the neurotransmitters, they use. The seemingly dry facts came to life, and Mark could feel the surge of adrenalin. His talk was not only routine passing on of knowledge to a dozen young men and women but became also a tribute to the pinnacle of evolution: the human brain.

As never before at an informal seminar, he was slightly nervous. But today's occasion was different from all the others and his audience was not the average medical student. A great deal was at stake: he was laying the ground for a novel set of experiments involving modifications of thought processing and influencing intentions. Under no circumstance should he fail his students. He was determined to confirm their commitment to the project: it would be a failure if any of them opted out of the series of tests.

Although the room was in semi-darkness, he could sense that the students' attention was focused on him, and even Maria, who had heard him before giving a seminar on this topic, was listening with special alertness.

'Do you know what its function is?' Waiting just a couple of seconds, as the students remained silent, Mark continued: 'We have known for some time that this region of the brain is involved in higher cognitive function. But before we go any further, we should look at the real thing.' The lights came on and Mark led the students from the seminar room to the adjacent laboratory, followed by Maria.

The demonstration room was as clean as an operating theatre. The similarity was increased by the centrally placed stainless steel table illuminated by a powerful lamp similar to those seen in surgical practice. On the table John Ibori, one of the research assistants, had already prepared one of the control brains. Despite the efficient extracting system a faint smell of formalin lingered over the table. When John noticed that a few of the students, not accustomed to the strong smell, grimaced and screwed up their noses, he handed out face masks. Only a couple bothered to put them on.

Mark picked up a pair of surgical gloves, slid his hands into them and, removing the brain from the table, guided his students over the most important structures. Now and again he asked one of the students to identify areas he specified with his index finger. He finished this tour at the frontal pole of the brain, outlining clearly the regions they were going to study in more detail.

'Why is this region of particular importance? The answer lies in a set of experiments carried out some time ago using functional imaging. This technique, functional magnetic resonance imaging, can reveal the activity of various brain regions. It has indicated that hidden intentions of the human brain can be read in this area.' The students stood around the demonstrating table in silence, intrigued.

'You might argue that the knowledge of these anatomical details is of no importance – they're not only boring but also a waste of time. Nothing of the sort. They provide the key to unlocking the secrets of higher cognitive functions. To understanding how thoughts are processed. And ultimately, how they can be modified.' He paused for a second: the students followed his every word.

'To test whether *hidden* intention can be revealed, volunteers were asked to select freely and perform one of two possible tasks – addition or subtraction. Using high-precision functional magnetic resonance imaging it was possible to determine the covert intention the subjects had previously chosen. To put it simply, in this experiment the scientists devised a system that can analyse brain activity to reveal the intentions of a person even before he or she acts upon them. From this, further experiments followed. Sophisticated computer systems can learn unique patterns or signatures of brain activity that correspond to different thoughts. By scanning the brain for these signatures, it can then be predicted what the person might be thinking. We can now, to some extent, read the human mind and predict intentions. At this stage, do you have any questions?' As the students remained silent, Mark added: 'Let's go down to imaging.'

The functional MRI Unit was in the basement of the building. Unlike other similar underground laboratories, this was a well-lit airy floor with the luxury of a relatively high ceiling. The bank of screens hanging from the ceiling was connected to the imaging laboratories and relayed pictures to the students who could follow the experiments sitting in their chairs. The imaging suites opened from a wide central corridor and each consisted of a small reception area with lockers, the anteroom with the bank of computers and the imaging room itself which housed the scanner.

As they settled down in the reception area, Mark gave a brief description of today's pilot experiment. He could hardly hide his impatience to start. Yet he stopped for a second. The outcome of what was going to happen within the next hour or so would be of vital importance not only for this particular project but also for his whole future career. Months of preparatory hard work would be put to the test: the first preliminary experiment was going to be crucial. The students, perceiving the significance of the experiments, watched him, holding their breath.

'Earlier we talked about how hidden intentions could be detected by functional imaging. In this pilot test we can also try to modify your secret aims. The experimental paradigm is simple. We select holiday destinations all over the world to see whether we can change your mind about where you want to go. Who volunteers first?' Several hands went up and, not to show favour, he picked the student nearest to him. Adrian was a tall slim boy who had the second highest IQ in the group.

'Follow me,' said Mark and they disappeared into the second imaging suite on the right-hand side of the corridor. Mark switched the camera on, so that the students with Maria could both hear and see them in the large reception area.

'Just for the sake of formality, I should confirm,' Mark turned to the student, 'that you haven't taken any drugs or alcohol during the last twenty-four hours?' Even the students' diet and water intake were regulated.

Mark had insisted that the preliminary experiments should be carried out in an atmosphere of confidentiality. It was not just the scientist's paranoia of competition, of which clearly there was no shortage – over the last couple of decades the understanding of the molecular basis of higher mental functioning had progressed with unprecedented speed – but Mark's concern lay in an entirely different direction. He was fully aware that if the nature of his experiments found its way prematurely into the media, it would create a sensation that could easily backfire. In this fast-moving field facts could easily be distorted. "Scientists now control your thoughts!" was not a headline he wanted to see.

They emptied their pockets of coins and removed their watches into plastic trays. Adrian also took off his wide leather belt with a large, ornate buckle.

On the large flat screen in front of them the title of the experiment appeared: "Changing Holiday Destinations."

'For the test we've selected eighty holiday destinations. You should imagine having a great time in these places. While you're lying in the scan, the names will be flashed up on the screen in pairs and you've to decide which one of the two destinations you prefer. Okay? If you're ready, let's go, but first remove your shoes,' said Mark. MAGNET ON declared a red sign and Mark pushed back the sliding door, ushering Adrian in front of him.

As he entered the room, with the student in tow, his nightmare, forgotten and buried by subsequent events of the day, flooded back for a second. Suddenly he realised that the imaging suite, which appeared so terrifying in the night, was none other than this very laboratory. But the threat of the stillness and silence of the nightmare had been replaced by animation and the background buzz of life. To his relief, it was all different and he took comfort in the familiarity of his daily environment. Only the massive equipment, creamy white and dominating the centre of the room was similar, but its bore, the short central cavity, was different from the endless dark tunnel of last night's vision into which he had disappeared.

Closing his mind to any further reflection, he was poised to start the experiment.

'Have you been screened before?' asked Mark and when he saw Adrian nodding he added: 'So you know the score. Hop on the bed.'

He put a sculpted foam rest under Adrian's knees and handed him two plastic earplugs to keep off the worst of the noise generated by the equipment. Once these were firmly in place, he helped Adrian to put on the headphones through which they were going to communicate during the experiment. Then he lifted the magnetic coil and clicked it into place to make contact with the other part of the circuit that was acting like a headrest: in doing so he established the magnetic field around Adrian's head. He adjusted the mirror that reflected the screen at the end of the bore.

'Are you ready?' asked Mark and when Adrian answered with a 'yes', he pushed back the joystick of the control: 'Here we go,' and the tray-like bed silently slid into the bore of the machine.

'Relax.' Mark spoke into the microphone and at that moment the three-dimensional image of Adrian's brain appeared on the monitor. 'We'll start the experiment.' On another screen he could follow the holiday destinations, as Adrian would see them in the scanner, making his choices.

'Before we start the final part of the experiment, you have a couple of minutes to relax. Think of nothing, just fix your eyes on the cross in the centre of the screen to allow us to scan the baseline activity of your brain.' After a short break, Mark continued: 'Then we are going to repeat the test, exactly the same way, but I'll attempt to manipulate the nerve cell circuitries which are involved in this particular decision-making. This external intervention, I can assure you, lasts only for the duration of the experiment and doesn't leave any permanent imprints in your brain.'

Presently, Mark fed the template into the computer. It was the most complex reconstruction of the pathways of the brain in existence, demonstrating relay centres and cortical target areas. He could barely hide his excitement. Within a few minutes he would see the results of protracted preparations. On a blank screen the neuronal networks of Adrian's brain lit up against the template. First he surveyed the entire map before zooming to the frontal pole.

In the complex marshalling yards of networks, he could control the electric impulses and the subsequent release of neurotransmitters. He could inhibit, block or stimulate transmission between nerve cells and was thus able to determine the final destination of impulses in the brain. For the duration of the experiment he was the master of Adrian's brain.

Simultaneously, another monitor came alive, recording the electrical activity of the student's brain: this new electroencephalogram could document the activity not only of a small region of the brain but also that of well-defined neuronal circuitries. These recordings progressed synchronously with those of the scanner. As the test got under way, it became obvious that Mark could influence the student's decision at will. In all but one case the original choice was reversed.

Mark drew a deep breath and then slowly exhaled a sigh of relief. The trial run was a success: months of planning had borne its fruit. The results on the screens were irrefutable evidence that intentions can be reversed. He had experienced success before: in school, at university and more recently in his professional life. Yet today's experiment was different. The exhilarating promise of a positive beginning and the tantalising bait of the result of a single test had urged him to proceed. Reproducing the results in the rest of the preliminary cohort, he thought, would certainly ensure further funding. And then by recruiting volunteers the real work could start. For a second he forgot that Adrian was still in the scanner.

'Well done,' he said and shook the student's hand before rejoining the others. The students were agitated, but as he approached them unexpectedly a hushed silence fell: they were impressed by the unqualified success of the experiment. Maria shook his hand:

'Congratulations,' but Mark interrupted her: 'These are early days for celebrations. If all the twelve preliminary tests come up with the same positive results, we'll be in a strong position to embark on a large-scale study. In the end we might learn more about neuronal circuitries which control human behaviour.'

'Yes, but the potential is far greater, don't you think?' Maria said, perhaps for the benefit of the watching students. 'You shouldn't be so self-effacing. This is perhaps the last stage in the understanding of how the human brain works. The crowning triumph of centuries of studies and discoveries: the final missing pieces of the jigsaw are beginning to fall into place.' Maria's enthusiasm knew no bounds: even decades of living in England could not completely bleach out her Latin temperament. Mark, barely able to hide his embarrassment, did not respond but threw an imploring glance at his colleague to shut her up. Then he addressed the students.

'Today we don't have any more screenings but from Thursday we'll do two each day – one in the morning and one in the after-noon. I will draw up the list and Catherine, my secretary, will contact you one by one with the date and time. We will finish the preliminary run early next week and the results can be analysed immediately afterwards. I'm sure you understand, but may I remind you again that you shouldn't communicate with anybody about these experiments until further notice?' The students and Maria shuffled out of the imaging suite: the lift door silently closed behind them. He was now on his own in the empty room.

Mixed with the sense of elation a tinge of doubt crept in insid-iously and unexpectedly. The experiments heralded a break-through, giving scientists unprecedented power similar to that of cloning human beings. To create life and to control human thoughts were the ultimate power of science. An instrument to be used for good. But also for evil. Suddenly, he could foresee all the potential difficulties of his success. But couldn't he be happy without any troubling thought just for a minute?

He heard people shuffling in the adjacent imaging suite, a distant telephone rang, the footsteps of a couple of PhD stu-dents, disgorged from the lift, died down in the corridor. As she passed his room, the Ethiopian physicist whose gazelle-like beauty he secretly admired but whose name he could not remember, collected iced-water from the fountain next to his door. For a minute he wanted to escape. He sat down in one of the leather swivel chairs and closed his eyes to empty his mind.

It was at this moment that Catherine's face appeared on a monitor, announcing in a clipped voice: 'Dr Chadwick, you have a visitor. Please come to your office as soon as you finish.'

The call jolted him out of his peace. He hadn't been expecting visitors. His annoyance was mixed with apprehension as he
closed the door of the imaging suite behind him to hurry back
to his office.

4

Mark walked towards the visitor with an outstretched right arm, ready for a handshake. In front of him stood a man of about his age or perhaps a couple of years older, elegantly dressed in a charcoal grey, pin-striped suit and wearing a dusty pink shirt with a heavy pink silk tie of a tiny purple and black pattern. Savile Row and Jermyn Street, Mark concluded, assessing his visitor, and then glancing at the immaculate black brogue shoes, hand-stitched at Lobb or at least Church's.

He could be a Harley Street consultant, he reflected, but the overall effect, however smart, was a touch too sharp for a medic. Unlike some of his colleagues whose studied shabbiness he disapproved of, Mark was himself a smart dresser, yet his visitor's elegance was at least a class above his standard, which did not extend beyond Jaeger or Austin Reed. There was, however, one common feature of their sartorial style: they both seemed to prefer English to continental clothing. Moreover, there was something too disciplined, if not straightforwardly military, about the bearing of the man standing before him.

They shook hands.

'Dr Robert Dufresne,' announced the visitor as if he were advertising a supreme brand.

'Please sit down, Dr Dufresne,' said Mark, pointing to the armchair nearest to his desk. 'Would you like some coffee?'

'Yes, thank you. Black no sugar,' said Dufresne. A polite request, yet it sounded like a command. While they were waiting for Catherine to bring the coffee, the visitor stood up, walked to the window and, looking at the panorama, could not suppress his spontaneous admiration.

'What a fantastic view! Driving here one doesn't appreciate that Denmark Hill is quite a climb. Lucky fellow having an office like this.' The familiarity, with which Dufresne was walking around in his office, had unsettled Mark and he remained silent. There was a knock on the door and Catherine appeared with the coffee: a tray of two cups and saucers and, on a matching plate, a few of Mark's favourite plain oatmeal biscuits.

'Excellent coffee,' complimented the visitor as they settled back into their chairs.

'What can I do for you, Dr Dufresne?' asked Mark. 'We haven't met before, have we?' As he uttered these words and their eyes met, he became less certain for a moment. On second scrutiny, the visitor's face was vaguely familiar. He must have seen him somewhere, but could not recall the place or the context.

'My name is Robert,' Dufresne said. 'May I call you Mark?'

You may not, he wanted to say, we don't know each other and I don't like strangers calling me by my first name. For him, maintaining an element of formality was not just protection from unwanted familiarity and meaningless intimacy, but also a more subtle gauge of communication. He could barely suppress a smile, remembering a recently overheard exchange between a nurse and an elderly patient: the nurse solicitously enquiring whether she could address her charge as Liz or Betty, to which the chilly answer was: 'You may call me Lady Morrison.' Nonetheless, he thought that an objection would have been both churlish and impolite.

'Yes, of course,' he replied, instantaneously despising himself for doing something, however unimportant, against his will. And, as if reading Mark's previous thought, Dufresne gave some information that did not come as a complete surprise.

'From the way you measured me up a few minutes ago, I am sure you realised that despite the title I am not,' the visitor was putting a strong emphasis on the last three words, 'a medical doctor. My PhD is in Modern History. I don't belong to the fraternity and I don't seem to have those distinguishing features by which members of the same tribe, like species in the animal kingdom, recognise each other.'

What a pompous ass, thought Mark.

'The way you sized me up I knew I couldn't fool you even if I wanted.'

It was at this moment that Mark's attitude towards the visitor grew more suspicious. The superficial, benevolent curiosity and the ready-made charitable 'can-I-help-you' attitude, ingrained into his profession to become his default position, were switched off. A yet hidden, but potentially dangerous game was to be played out on this peaceful late October afternoon. There was a pause. Dufresne was slowly approaching the purpose of his visit.

'By now you might have guessed,' said the visitor, smiling but with a touch of irony, 'that I work for the security services.' With a sudden click of recognition Mark remembered the media speculations following the appointment of someone unknown and relatively young to become one of the senior officers of a massive force responsible for the security of London within the newly created Department of Home Security.

'We know your international reputation, your papers in leading medical and scientific journals, including those in *Nature, Science, The Lancet, The New England Journal of Medicine, The Proceedings of the National Academy of Sciences of the United States*, etc, etc., to mention just a few. We have just seen a preview of the documentary about your work prepared for the BBC's Science Channel.'

Mark was now barely surprised that his guest knew not only the existence of, but had also had access to, the unreleased sixty-minute documentary which was being kept strictly under wraps until its planned release the following month. However, he was astonished that Dufresne had taken the trouble to arrange a screening in the morning before he came to see him. He could not help admiring the thoroughness with which Dufresne had obviously prepared for their encounter. He did not know that the BBC had already projected the film on one of the screens at the Headquarters of Home Security on the Embankment.

'I was never much good at biological sciences and know even less about neuroscience,' confessed the visitor. 'The report was illuminating, but could you explain to me exactly what you do? Just in a few sentences to be easily understandable for a layman.'

That is what the film was doing and I am sure you have a very good idea of the nature of our work, reflected Mark but he obliged by repeating the mission statement of the Institute: 'We study cognitive functions in order to understand how the brain works. We try to correlate expressions of social emotions like compassion, shame and guilt and moral judgements unique to man with specialised areas of the brain. We can now do this by high resolution functional imaging of the neural networks of the brain based on specialised computer technology.' At this point Mark sensed that he might get carried away but, controlling his enthusiasm, he stopped.

'Could you give us an example?' Dufresne asked. Mark hesitated for a moment, but then he continued.

'This is an age-old paradigm which has been entertaining classes of moral philosophy for some time. The problem is known as the runaway railway carriage paradox. The runaway carriage, if nothing is done, will kill five people further down the line. However, they can be saved by setting the points to shunt the carriage to a siding where it will kill one person. Should one set the points?'

Dufresne listened attentively, as Mark, not expecting an answer, continued: 'In a different version of the paradox the only way to save the five people is by pushing someone deliberately in front of the train. Should one kill an innocent man? In both cases the outcome is the same – one bystander has to perish in order to spare five, yet the responses they evoke are very different. While most people have no difficulty in setting the points; the decision in the second version is more controversial, since it is complicated by feelings of guilt. However, people who have suffered damage to a particular brain area that contains the moral decision module can make this decision with ease. Thus, one can argue that making a certain moral decision is associated with a well-defined area of the brain.'

'Are you saying,' Dufresne interjected, 'that by studying brain anatomy you will understand the way brain mechanisms produce behavioural patterns?'

'Exactly. Using sophisticated methods of brain imaging we are in the process of constructing a map of brain functions which we then can correlate with behavioural patterns.'

'Fascinating,' said Dufresne looking down at the back of his hands, carefully studying his nails. And then without any introduction: 'Do you know a certain Fiona Cartwright?' As he posed the question, Dufresne pushed his chair closer to Mark – so that they were now sitting equidistant from the desk – and at the same time leaned forward. This move unexpectedly shifted the balance of power in the room – the visitor became the interrogator.

For the first time, in Dufresne's steely purpose, barely hidden under the cloak of studied mannerisms, Mark perceived the undercurrent of a deeper running threat that had yet to surface. The hard-edged ruthlessness could cut through the thin veneer of civilised behaviour at any time. Mark tried to relax, but his body would not obey. His mouth had dried up. His muscles grew tense. He focused his gaze on the visitor's face.

For a second he hesitated.

'Yes, Fiona Cartwright is one of my patients. You probably already know that she is. If so, why bother to ask?' Dufresne nodded. 'You must know,' Mark continued, 'that it would be improper for me to discuss her medical condition with you.'

'Of course, of course, the Hippocratic oath, the medical confidentiality,' responded Dufresne with barely hidden sarcasm. 'In the interest of the patients. That convenient little cloak to give trust and dignity to the profession even in cases when none is deserved. To cover up malpractices, greed and lies.'

Mark stared at Dufresne with disbelief. He had not antici-
pated that they would arrive at an open confrontation after such
a short time. With such a cheap and vulgar attack on the medical
profession.

'Does your outburst mean that medical confidentiality repre-
sents a security risk in this case?'

'Look, Mark,' said Dufresne in a conciliatory tone, 'there is
no need for you to break medical confidentiality. You may not
be aware, but I have the authority to read the medical records
of all your patients, should I decide to do so, however confidential they might be. I can also have access to scrutinise just
about every other aspect of their lives, including their criminal
records, if they have any, their bank statements, the names of
their lovers, when they jumped a red light, where they spend
their holiday, where they shop, which film they saw recently and
occasionally, should my curiosity in the name of security extend
that far, what they had for dinner.'

There was a silence which neither of them wanted to break.
Mark struggled to hide his revulsion. Suddenly he wished he
could abscond from his own office and leave the visitor behind.
After a few seconds that seemed unnaturally long, Dufresne
spoke with his voice becoming mellower.

'Mark, you can stop worrying about medical confidentiality. Fiona Cartwright is not one of your patients anymore.' He
paused for a second for effect and then he added in a matter-of-
fact style without emphasis or sentiment:

'She is dead.'

5

Enjoying the freshness of the autumn weather, Yasmina decided to walk to the British Library. She could not help thinking of Mark. She knew intuitively that this morning he was starting the most important chapter of his career. The significance of his experiments was all too obvious even for a layman. She wished him success. Yet somehow she could not suppress the feeling that there was an element of competition between them. Just the other day Mark had accused her, half teasingly, half seriously, of being jealous of his rapid progression on the academic ladder. Occasionally she resented that Mark regarded her as a solid platform, a support system for his advancement rather than an equal partner. This brought out the rebel in her and she was determined to make her reputation in modern history in her own right.

Passing in front of the houses of Chester Terrace, she banished these disturbing thoughts, and from the serenity of the park she resurfaced into the noise of the fast-flowing traffic of Albany Street. This was one of the many fault lines of London where two completely different worlds met: here the classical elegance and obvious, yet understated affluence of Regent's Park collided with the tenements of a council estate. So near, yet so far: separated by only a few yards, these neighbours were living poles apart, inhabiting a different universe.

From a distance she could hear the demented barking of the siren of a police car speeding towards Euston with its light flashing. As she turned into Robert Street she came across young mothers who were accompanying their children to school. They were nearly all black or Asian. Hardly any white children. The atmosphere was sullen: no sign of camaraderie, no smiles and no friendly greetings. Several Muslim women wore headscarves; under a new law these were allowed but the burqua had been banned a long time ago for security reasons.

Crossing the road, she heard a child crying out. She slowed her steps and turned around. A few yards behind her a small girl of five or six was lying on the pavement. The wheels of her bicycle were still turning. Yasmina rushed to her and as she picked her up, the girl stopped crying and looked at her with wet uncomprehending eyes. She felt a surge of warmth and was about to ask whether she had hurt herself when the mother appeared on the scene, breathless. She was trailing a smaller boy behind her. An attractive Asian woman dressed in black, wearing a headscarf and heavily pregnant. Ignoring Yasmina, she turned to the little girl.

'I did warn you – you should remain at my side! I turn away for a second and you cycle away like crazy. Don't ever do it again!' Her presence still unacknowledged, Yasmina wanted to compliment the mother on the beauty of her daughter but chose to remain silent. She felt rejection and even dislike emanating from this unknown woman whom she had never seen before. The stranger resented her, and the help she spontaneously offered was probably deemed to be an intrusion into her hermetic world. Lifting the bicycle, the woman finally said, barely looking at her: 'Thank you,' and ushered the girl away.

Walking in these streets Yasmina was seized by uncertainty. As a fully emancipated, well-educated woman she was firmly anchored to the Western system of moral values and social mores, yet the land of her father still held fascination for her. In her late teens she had succumbed to the seduction and spent six months travelling in India, trying to discover the ancestral home of her forefathers who had left Gujarat at the turn of the twentieth century.

She had been brought up as a Muslim, yet during summer vacations, visiting her mother's parents in Prague, she had encountered a different faith. Her Czech grandparents were religious Catholics who, although agreeing to it at the time, could never completely accept their daughter's conversion to Islam. It was Yasmina who demanded to be taken to their local church. She was overwhelmed by the harmony of the baroque architecture, the richness of the decorations, the smell of incense, the flickering candles, the pictures which spoke of both suffering and ecstasy, and the music, which she later learned was a Bach toccata, played by an unseen organist.

When she joined Mark to live with him in Cambridge Place, her father, Wahid, did not protest about his daughter setting up home with a non-Muslim, and her mother, Jana, could barely hide her satisfaction: life coming full circle. Yasmina lived on the cusp of two worlds, yet belonged to neither.

After passing Euston Station, the final leg of the walk took Yasmina towards the completely regenerated King's Cross area. The British Library had been for a long time an isolated temple of culture in the neighbourhood of three railway termini, an area where people were in continuous transit.

She entered the portico gate from Euston Road and hurriedly crossed the piazza, glancing at the monumental bronze figure of Newton. Once inside the building she felt at home. Natural light, harmony of space, exquisite materials and attention to detail. The atmosphere of the library reminded her of her own contribution, although she did not have any illusion about her current research surviving for centuries. It was far too ephemeral; 'glorified journalism', she used to say in one of her deprecatory moods. But these were only fleeting moments, since she was convinced that the investigations of the role of Islamic extremism, as a contributing factor in creating a centralised state, were worth pursuing. She was determined to carve out a successful academic career in modern history. Deep down she inherited the will and enterprising spirit of her Indian grandfather who arrived dispossessed from Idi Amin's Uganda in the early 1970s to become a successful businessman in catering.

The Humanities Reading Room, on all three floors, was unusually busy this morning. She entered the lowest level, a space flooded with light. Many desks were already occupied – students working on their degrees, trainee journalists checking facts, pensioners for whom books were their only company of the day. At the reception desk she was greeted by Rosemary, her favourite junior librarian. She had ebony skin, pleated hair and dazzling teeth. These came into their own during one of her infectious laughs, which she occasionally had to tone down as some of the readers, having been disturbed by the noise, looked up from their books, throwing disapproving glances at her.

'Rosemary, when Mr Khan arrives, please send him straight to my office. Thanks.'

Ted Khan was Yasmina's PhD student, a bright young man in his early twenties. He shone out amongst the dozen candidates who had applied for the PhD scholarship, and the interviewing panel unanimously agreed to offer the studentship to him. Even Barry Henshaw, Yasmina's boss, who initially favoured one of the female applicants gave in and dropped his candidate in favour of Ted at the final round of discussions. Their meeting was scheduled to be in one of the offices at the back of the library, facing the side of St Pancras Station. It was a small room and shared by several colleagues who, like Yasmina, were seconded to the Library for their research projects. Here she did not need much space since her permanent office in which she kept most of her books and files was in University College across Euston Road.

Presently, there was a knock on the door and Ted Khan entered: a tall, lanky figure with long dark hair and dark brown eyes, only pockmarks on his face spoiling his fine features. He was wearing jeans, a light green corduroy shirt and a loose white sweater. Greeting Yasmina, he said without any introduction: 'You heard about the shooting in the stadium.' It was a statement rather than a question and Yasmina nodded; she had picked up fragments of conversations on her way to the office. However, she was disinclined to rake over yesterday's events: she was rather looking forward to the planned discussion of Ted's project.

'Coffee?' she asked. Without waiting for a reply, she prepared two mugs of coffee. 'Did you have time to read the references I gave you last time?' From their initial meetings she had been convinced that Ted would produce his own ideas and become one of those students who would propel his PhD work without much prodding, and whose supervision after a while would turn into a mutual exchange of ideas. And Ted did not need much prompting.

'The Government used the most recent terrorist outrages to assume absolute power and to build up the Surveillance State that we now know. The chaos in the wake of the recent bombings was the final excuse, which was handed on a plate by the terrorists. Furthermore, one can't exclude the possibility that the reason why the Government didn't clamp down more drastically on extremist organisations and turned a blind eye to their activities was to allow terrorist attacks so horrifying that no one could object to the declaration of a State of Emergency. This transitory period after the bombings was exploited by the Government to acquire sweeping powers.'

'Do you think we will be popular with this message? It will be delivered by a project sponsored by the government after all.'

'I don't think that Home Security will be much concerned about a PhD project.'

I wouldn't be so sure, she mused. She did not tell Ted that all the higher degree theses together with all the publications on social and political sciences went on a central computer containing information on university staff. Mark had told her that, as from the beginning of the year, published results in the field of neuroscience, particularly those in higher cognitive function, behaviour, emotion and memory were now centrally recorded. Ted, not noticing Yasmina's unease, continued: 'The worst that can happen is that the results of my thesis won't be published.' If we are lucky, thought Yasmina, but she faced the challenge with excitement.

'What is the timescale for reviewing Islamist extremism? From 7 July 2005? It would be a dramatic starting point.'

On that day, as even younger generations remembered, suicide bombers had killed fifty-two people travelling on underground trains and a double-decker bus. The most horrifying aspect was that the terrorists who brought mass murder and chaos into the centre of London were not foreign nationals but young Britons. An uncomprehending public was astonished when they realised that the hatred their fellow citizens harboured for them ran so deep that they were prepared to kill themselves in the attempt.

Ted hesitated for a few seconds: 'Yes, this is a possibility but we could have an alternative. I think we might have a better date: 14 January 1989.'

Since Yasmina looked at him vacantly, he added just one word as if helping her memory in a quiz.

'Bradford.'

Suddenly everything fell into place. For Yasmina remembered the Salman Rushdie business. The publication of a book, a seemingly insignificant everyday event in a country where tens of thousands of books flooded the shops every year, had exploded into a major international affair. The book caused worldwide demonstrations, scores of deaths around the world and Ayatollah Khomeini, the Supreme Leader of Iran at the time, issued a fatwa to kill the author who was the citizen of another sovereign country, ignoring all subsequent diplomatic complications. In British society, the incident had created a hitherto novel type of social conflict. Already a well-known author at the time and himself a Muslim, Rushdie's book, entitled *The Satanic Verses*, was deemed blasphemous by Muslims. In the ensuing mayhem a little remembered event occurred in the northern English town of Bradford. A chanting mob burnt the book, although few, if any, had read the allegedly offending text.

'Or we could start with an even earlier date of 2 December 1988, when an estimated 7,000 Muslims demonstrated in Bolton and burnt the book, but somehow the events in Bradford created more publicity. One of these is a good date to start the review of the history of recent terrorism,' added Ted. 'Burning books has historical significance. The Nazis burnt the books of Jewish authors. And we know where that hatred led.'

Yasmina nodded in agreement. From her course on European fascism between the two world wars, she recalled a quotation from Heine and was happy to share it with Ted: '"Where one burns books, one will, in the end, burn people."'

'And people do nothing to prevent it. By the way, Yasmina, I should have mentioned it earlier that last week we had a visit from Home Security in the college. It was well advertised and the main auditorium was overflowing. I think their aim was to make the service attractive, and at the same time to counter what they see as the universities being the breeding ground of terrorism and anarchy.'

'Interesting,' said Yasmina, remembering a similar occasion when she was a student – they had tried to recruit her. Being a Muslim and half-Asian she was an ideal candidate. 'Did they approach you after the meeting?'

'No, they didn't. But I must say that the officer who gave the talk was brilliant – crystal clear and sharp.'

'Do you remember his name?' When Ted recalled it, the name meant absolutely nothing to her.

6

Mark pushed his chair back from the desk as if attempting to distance himself from Dufresne. Although shocked and surprised, he was not prepared to betray his feelings.

'What happened?' he asked, looking straight into the eyes of his visitor. Dufresne did not answer, but with barely hidden irritation in his voice he asked:

'You must have heard what happened in the stadium yesterday?' and since Mark did not respond, he added with a mixture of annoyance and incredulity: 'Perhaps I should tell you a little bit more, particularly as Fiona Cartwright was one of your patients. One could argue, couldn't one,' and his tone became more emphatic, 'that even if you were not responsible for her actions, her well-being was certainly your responsibility. If she was under your care, as indeed she was.'

Listening to Dufresne, the full horror of what had happened in the stadium the day before gradually dawned on Mark. And when it did, the realisation struck him with elementary force. Dufresne could not fail to notice the sudden shift in Mark's mood and wasted no time in exploiting his adversary's momentary weakness.

'You are surprised, aren't you, that a decent professional middle-class woman is prepared to commit murder? Even worse – to kill a public figure! And for you, as a psychiatrist, the shock is even more painful. It hurts your professional pride. The belief that you know your patient!'

'It can't be right,' Mark blurted out. But Dufresne continued remorselessly. Her name was not going to be released until her family had been informed. Nor was the security officer involved in the affair to be identified. Nonetheless, Dufresne made it perfectly clear that, in the tersely worded communiqué in the official bulletin as well as in all the media outlets, careful emphasis was made of the fact of her being under psychiatric treatment.

She must have been deranged: this view took the wind out of the sail of rumours, which the Government wanted to suppress by any means, that her desperate act might have been an expression of resistance to the Government's increasing control of the population. However, to Mark's relief, it appeared that the hospital in which she had undergone treatment was not named.

Silently, Mark had to accept that his guest's description was masterly. He felt as if he had been in the stadium, witnessing the event. It was atmospheric, yet without any unnecessary embellishments. If Mark had any doubts whether Fiona was the person who had attempted to shoot the President, listening to Dufresne's portrayal of the would-be assassin had expelled the last shred of uncertainty. The smartly dressed woman with a gun in her hand was his patient.

He stood up and, without looking at Dufresne, slowly walked to the window. Silent and motionless, he ignored his visitor before returning to his desk. He sat down, keyed in his personal code and called up his patients' database. Then he typed in Fiona Cartwright's name. He still didn't say anything. There was no need to talk: Dufresne knew exactly what he was doing. He opened Fiona's file. Even though she was dead and he could no longer help her, Mark was still reluctant to lay bare her life on the screen, to share it with a stranger. Scrolling the screen, he read out in a lifeless voice, first in staccato then more fluently, Fiona Cartwright's history.

'Born 27 November 1992. Only child of a middle-class family. Father a civil servant. Mother an English teacher at Camden School for Girls. A self-contained and distant woman. No close bond with her daughter. Their relationship deteriorated when Fiona found out as a teenager that her mother was having an affair with one of her colleagues at school. They only reconciled when her mother was dying of ovarian cancer.' A picture of Fiona's serious face came to Mark's mind.

'Her father became an incidental victim of gang warfare. He was caught up in an exchange of gunfire between a teenage gang of drug dealers and the police. He was hit by a single bullet and died on the way to the hospital. This was the beginning of Fiona's psychiatric history – a deep depression from which she never completely recovered.' Uttering these words, Mark realised just how deeply the unexpected loss of Fiona had affected him; during their sessions he had begun not only to appreciate but even to like her troubled yet straightforward and thoroughly decent character.

'Which year did this happen?' Dufresne interjected.

'It must have been in 2011 – the year she was about to start law at Bristol. She had a poor attendance record during the first term but she rallied to graduate with an upper second degree.'

'Did she have any close friends at university? Someone who might have had a strong influence on her? Whose political views she might have found attractive?' Dufresne asked. For some reason Mark found himself reluctant to cooperate wholeheartedly with his visitor.

'Not as far as we know. Anyway, there's nothing in the records which would suggest that she might have fallen under the spell of an extremist group.' Even before he could finish the last sentence, he suddenly remembered a conversation, which, thinking it irrelevant at the time, he had not recorded. And now, he was not going to share it with Dufresne. As if nothing had happened, he continued: 'When she got back to London, she rented a small flat in Maida Vale and joined a City firm. Then she got a job in Selfridge's where she dealt with customer complaints.'

Obscurely, he hoped that concentrating on the bare facts of Fiona's CV would discourage Dufresne from further probing questions. He felt, somehow, that he needed to protect her. But Dufresne persisted.

'Anything about her private life? Affairs? She must have had some fun outside work. She was once a young woman – not exactly a beauty but quite attractive.'

Instinctively again, Mark distrusted Dufresne's motives for asking so many questions. He knew Dufresne had a job to do and he wondered at his disinclination to tell him everything.

'As a trainee solicitor she had a stable boyfriend who was a fellow solicitor specialising in maritime law. He was eager to marry her. But soon after she had turned him down their relationship broke up. Since then she had only had a handful of short-term affairs, and it was usually she who called it a day.'

Dufresne changed the subject: 'I'm not interested in her actual medication, but could you tell me when her treatment started?' Before answering, Mark could not suppress his doubt that Dufresne already knew more about Cartwright than he did. As if reading his thoughts, Dufresne added: 'We've already compiled a detailed file on her, but our early records, how shall I put it, are far from complete.' At this admission Mark could not suppress a smile, but nevertheless he continued to read his notes, abbreviating and paraphrasing here and there.

'Her spates of depression became longer and more serious. Typically, she hesitated for a long time before seeking medical advice but eventually she was asked whether she would agree to participate in an experimental trial conducted here.'

While Mark was reading Fiona Cartwright's background, he did not look up from the screen, barely acknowledging the presence of Dufresne. He well remembered Fiona's first appointment: her initial reticence and then, as she gradually relaxed, her eagerness to unburden herself, to tell her story. During subsequent sessions, a rapport and mutual understanding had grown between them. She had talked freely about her hatred of the Surveillance State. Although she had nothing to hide, she had resented the institutionalised intrusion into her privacy. When Mark had questioned her about whether she should not be more appreciative of the extension of the National Government's power – which, after all, had put an end to the urban violence which had claimed her father – Fiona had remarked simply but with a sense of determination which had not left any space for compromise: 'It's far too high a price to pay for security.'

It had been on this occasion that Fiona had first mentioned a group of people whom she had recently encountered in the small seaside town of Whitstable in Kent, but Mark decided, again, not to elucidate this unrecorded conversation to Dufresne. The idea of their lifestyle, establishing some independence from the State, had appealed to Fiona and she had decided to travel to the seaside to visit these people and to witness their life. Even after a short visit, she had been captivated by what she experienced at first hand, and had been full of admiration and enthusiasm on her return. Her excursion took place well before nationwide publicity and the media had coined the term: Persons Without Identity or PWIs.

When Fiona had asked him point-blank whether he would find such a lifestyle attractive himself, Mark had been taken aback. He had felt that his patient's question was misguided: even if he had shared her political views, Fiona must have appreciated that his work could not be carried out in utopian isolation. He could not envisage joining such a group in rural Kent or anywhere. Fiona had trespassed on the well-defined but never articulated boundaries of their relationship and it had been presumptuous of her to assume that he would swap his career for a rural idyll. Instead of giving a straightforward answer, he had referred to his future plans and brought the conversation to an abrupt end.

Fiona had never raised this issue again but Mark suspected that his esteem in his patient's opinion had somehow diminished. When Mark had read the report by the analyst Fiona had been visiting separately at his recommendation, he agreed with the conclusion that the most likely root of her problems was the violent death of her father. Functional imaging had also confirmed this finding. When Fiona relived the events of her father's death, the pictures had shown consistent activation in the part of the brain that stores old memories. At this point, five months after the first appointment, Mark had suggested that she could enter treatment to suppress painful memories.

In Fiona Mark had found an ideal patient. The memories of her father's death had been obliterated in two stages: first the visual content of the memory and then the emotional content of the fatal night had been erased. The treatment had been nearing completion, and Fiona's last session with Mark had been scheduled for the following week. Looking at the screen, he deleted the appointment and instead typed as an epilogue to her troubled life: "Died 22 October 2040. Results of forensic post-mortem examination to follow."

Then he closed Fiona Cartwright's file.

7

'I have two further questions for you,' Dufresne declared. 'Do you think she intended to kill the President?'

'I don't know.' Then, recalibrating his answer: 'I am not sure.' He hesitated to tell Dufresne about Fiona Cartwright's attitude to the Surveillance State but with an irrepressible impulse he continued: 'My patient disapproved of some of the recent changes. She disliked the increasingly authoritarian power of the Government.' It was hatred, Mark would have liked to say but went on: 'The extension of the powers of the Surveillance State. The erosion of personal freedom.'

Dufresne interjected: 'You sound as if you were agreeing with her.'

Mark could not ignore the remark: 'Whether I do or not is entirely irrelevant to Cartwright's problem.' Observing the ironic tone in Dufresne's voice, he immediately regretted that he had taken the bait. He must not lose his temper. Then, he suddenly remembered something Fiona had mentioned. And he ignored it. Her nephew, an art student at the Courtauld Institute, with a flamboyant personality and anarchistic views had been arrested after a violent demonstration, taken to a police station and charged with disorderly behaviour. After his release, he had spent the first night in her flat and Fiona was incensed since she was convinced of the boy's innocence. Could this seemingly unimportant incident have triggered Fiona's tragic attempt? Mark was jolted back to the present by Dufresne's next question.

'Do you think you have failed your patient?' Dufresne pressed on.

Suddenly, Mark felt threatened. There were a few seconds of

silence. 'No, I don't. I hope you are not accusing me of medical negligence? I can only repeat what I said before. She didn't betray any obvious warning signs of an immediate breakdown. Something must have happened after her last appointment.' Dufresne nodded in acceptance and shifted his chair as if preparing to stand up. That didn't take long, thought Mark with relief. He wanted to be on his own to reflect on the whole history of his patient whose life had so dramatically and unexpectedly ended yesterday.

But to his irritation, Dufresne was not ready to finish. 'For some time, we've been following your work with interest. Our specialists at Headquarters have a very high opinion of your expertise. In the BBC documentary you went out of your way not to talk about one subject at any length. I understand that you even asked your volunteers to pledge themselves to secrecy. What's the fashionable term?' Dufresne paused as if searching for the correct expression but Mark knew that he was using this break to gauge his response.

Suddenly, there was renewed tension in the air. 'Oh, yes,' he continued, 'thought modification? Do we understand correctly that it's now possible to read people's intentions and then modify them? This programme could be of great interest to us. It has tremendous potential for increasing the security of the country. As you know, there are certain groups of people who are a threat to the security of the State. Religious fanatics. Terrorists. Dangerous criminals. Traitors. Foreign spies. Those who would not refrain from any action to destroy the stability and security of the country. People who would, at the first opportunity, bring back the chaos of the recent past rather than live in prosperity and peace. They are enemies of the State.'

Exploiting Dufresne's pause, Mark interjected: 'This is not going to happen for some time. The methodology is far from perfect. In the documentary we simply indicated that this is one avenue we could explore. And there is a long way from preliminary experiments to producing reliably consistent and reproducible results.'

Ignoring Mark's objection, Dufresne pursued his subject: 'More recently, we have also become interested in people who refuse to carry their Personal Identity Databases. They protest that these are in complete breach of their privacy. Perhaps I'm naïve, but if you don't have anything to hide, you shouldn't be concerned.'

That was a matter of opinion, Mark thought, but he remained silent. He himself strongly disliked the idea of being tagged, like an experimental animal, with Personal Identity Databases or PIDs but these chips had become a fact of life. Listening to his visitor, he cursed the minute he agreed to participate in the BBC documentary.

'In the first instance we are talking about a couple of dozen people, no more,' Dufresne continued, 'who are serious criminals and enemies of the State. If it's correct, what we found out about your work, that you can change or even influence intentions as you claim, then you can help. You could be of assistance not only to us but also to all these people who would otherwise be sent to prison.' The way Dufresne phrased his request did not leave any doubt that he and his colleagues in Home Security had known more than what they had gleaned from the documentary. Mark did not respond. The air froze around them. By now Dufresne was in his stride and continued relentlessly:

'You must see the advantages. Scientifically, you would have a unique cohort: the most challenging group of people for your experiments. They are far more interesting than your volunteers. Think of your boring medical students. What thoughts do they want to hide? If they have any thoughts at all! Consider all the exciting developments which might result from working with these people. Just think how you could change their lives for the better: from being subversive and destructive in our society to being supporters of the State, able to make positive contributions to the community. You could save them from prison. Collaborating with us is also not without considerable financial reward – we would pay for your research. Handsomely. We know that your current funding is under review. We would also make sure that you get all the money you need for the next five years. If you want to avoid being on our payroll for this work, we can channel our support through the Research Council.' He stopped, sitting back in the chair, waiting for the answer.

Mark remained silent. He had a feeling of increasing dread. A hard knot in his chest.

Dufresne continued: 'If you have doubts, can I give you one or two examples of the type of criminals we have in mind? A man in his late thirties who has spent most of his life in prison. Brought up by his mother, father unknown. From early childhood truancy he graduated to petty crimes and joined a gang in south London; kids still in their teens who terrorised the neighbourhood. One evening, they set upon a youth, who apparently belonged to a rival gang. They kicked him to death. Cameras showed that our man was the leader of the pack, and he was convicted of manslaughter. Having served six years of the sentence, he was released on parole. He didn't waste much time: he soon ganged up with one of his mates whom he had met in prison, and was involved in an armed robbery that went fatally wrong. Not far from where you live, in fact. They held up a couple as they returned home from the opera. At gunpoint they forced their way into their house to take all the contents of a safe. He shot the husband and when he could not remove a large diamond ring from the wife's hand, he cut off her finger.'

Mark felt a slight nausea. Dufresne pressed on, obviously exploiting his adversary's weakness: 'He was referred to us by the police since he'd also got involved in an international drug smuggling ring, funding terrorism. You wouldn't believe the range of criminals we have to deal with. They would be a gold mine for your studies. Unique material you wouldn't find easily anywhere else. We're offering them to you on a plate. Here's another, rather different example. A terrorist in his mid-twenties who attempted with three others to blow up the high security police station in south London. They didn't succeed but blew up their car to

escape arrest. He miraculously survived and on repeated interrogations didn't show the slightest remorse. On the contrary, he
confirmed over and over that he wouldn't hesitate to try it again.'

Presently, Dufresne paused dramatically and looked straight
into Mark's eyes: 'These are the people you can help.'

For a minute Mark remained silent. He could not ignore the
last sentence. Perhaps Dufresne was right: he could help these
people. Yet, he found the idea of Dufresne interfering with the
decision-making of the Health Sciences Research Council on
his behalf abhorrent. He knew what he was going to say but
waiting a little longer gave him an opportunity to run through
his argument.

'It is a generous offer,' Mark started, carefully weighing every
word, 'and I have to think about it. You must know the reasons
I can't accept your offer without hesitation. The first problem is
medical confidentiality, which your proposal would breach. We
couldn't tell the results of our investigations and treatment to
a third party without the permission of the patient. And more
importantly, we would be facing serious ethical problems. We
must have written consent from the individuals, declaring that
they agree to the tests: the nature of these has to be explained
before we can ask them to sign the declaration. The people you
have in mind are not volunteers: they would be giving their
consent under duress.'

Mark realised that this last sentence had placed him on a
confrontational course with his visitor. Dufresne's reply was
swift: 'We won't force these people to do anything. We'll simply
explain to them that it's in their own interest to collaborate with
us. It will be their choice to submit themselves to the tests in
your department.'

'What will their fate be if they refuse?' asked Mark.

'We would allow the law to take its usual course. They would
be investigated by Home Security or by the police, as appro-
priate, according to their crime, and if there were reasonable
grounds for an indictment they would be charged as necessary.'

'And you don't call this coercion?'

'Dr Chadwick,' Mark noted the shift from first name, 'you can call it whatever you wish. But I am sure that our stratagem would work. Most people would prefer a few visits to a brilliant psychiatrist rather than the near certainty of going through a criminal trial, and in many cases spending some time in prison. And can I put it to you more bluntly now? In the end we would get what we want in the interest of the State: law-abiding citizens. And you would also get what you want: scientific excitement by studying a challenging group of people and guaranteed funding for the next five years. This is a fair deal. Think it over before you say no. Perhaps you want to discuss it with your current partner, Yasmina, and also with your ex-wife, Anne Bennett, with your friend Daniel Weiss and, last but not least, with your grandfather James. Your grandmother, Clarissa, isn't in a position to give advice any more, is she?'

Dufresne stood up and looked at him. He lifted his right hand as if offering it for a handshake, but then unexpectedly aborted the move and lowered the outstretched hand as if anticipating that Mark would not reciprocate the gesture. 'Think it over, Dr Chadwick,' was Dufresne's parting shot, 'we will be in touch.'

From the half open door Dufresne turned back: 'We might even find a way to make our offer more attractive. Or alternatively you might conclude that you simply have no option but to accept.'

8

After Dufresne had left the room, Mark walked slowly to the window. As he stood motionless, the panorama of London, so ravishing earlier that morning, lost focus and became a blur: patches of colours randomly bleeding into each other without defining outlines. Although by now Dufresne was descending to the ground floor, his presence still lingered in the office and the leather armchair bore the contour of his body. Mark could still smell the faint fragrance of his aftershave. Inexplicably, he felt a bout of sudden queasiness and an urge to open the windows but they were all hermetically sealed and had to be shattered in case of emergency.

The shock of Fiona Cartwright's death weighed heavily upon him. He was responsible for her well-being and now he blamed himself for letting his patient down. He should have picked up some warning signs but there were none. At the same time he was desperately searching his mind to find out whether they had made a mistake in her treatment, yet he was convinced in the end that the care they provided was right. Dufresne was clearly going to exploit his patient's tragic death and would not hesitate to use this trump card against him, should he find it convenient. His parting line still rang clearly in his ear: '… you simply have no option but to accept.' Mark was not vain, but screaming headlines flashed through his mind: "Internationally known doctor neglected his patient." "Murder in the Stadium: mentally unstable woman killed during an unsuccessful attempt on the President's life."

Despite himself Mark's mind returned to the question at the heart of his dilemma. His visitor was right in one respect at least:

the individuals under criminal investigation would prove to be a unique cohort. He did not fool himself. He was faced with a once-in-a-lifetime opportunity, offered to him on a plate by Dufresne. Not even with all the resources he needed would he be able to recruit such an extraordinary collection of people. A gold mine of psychopathology; he couldn't have asked for more. He was torn between the challenge to his professional ability to change the lives of these people for the better and the revulsion he felt at Dufresne's offer.

Before doing anything else he wanted to talk to Yasmina. As he called her number, the screen appeared blank and instead of her face a curt message appeared: 'In the reading room until two thirty.'

He looked at his watch: it was five minutes past one already. Dufresne's visit had occupied nearly an hour of his time. He suddenly realised that he had also missed Hugh Cameron's seminar on the future of human evolution. This was unfortunate, Mark thought with genuine regret. Hugh Cameron was a controversial scientist whose public appearances, whether at prestigious lectures at international conferences or more run-of-the-mill seminars, always attracted large crowds. He was unapologetically arrogant, even by the standard of Cambridge's intellectual elite. A brilliant mind, effortlessly synthesising genetics with philosophy.

'Evolution is more complex than genetics filtered through time,' he used to tell his students and devoted his career to attacking current dogmas. In his more recent work he set out to explore catastrophic and random evolutionary events which could lead to gradual distraction of the results of biological evolution. To prevent this, he suggested, it would be necessary to control human evolution. This particular thesis had created controversy well beyond academia and launched a thousand polemics. Mark was certain that he had missed a stimulating hour but he knew that he must concentrate on more immediate problems now. He went through to Catherine, to see when he might see Blakemore.

As he entered her office, she was standing behind her desk, waiting for him. She had just finished proofreading Mark's latest paper to get it ready for his final check before despatching it to *Nature* to be published online the following week as one of the main articles with special editorial comments, emphasising the importance of his hypothesis on the mechanism in neuronal networks in thought processing. They looked at each other but neither of them mentioned the visitor.

The Director's office was on the top floor. Instead of calling the lift, Mark rushed up the emergency staircase, leaping two steps at a time. Gillian, Blakemore's secretary, was a jovial woman in her late thirties who, while discreet about her boss's professional affairs, was quite open about her private life in which boyfriends moved in and out with indecent frequency.

'Hi, Mark,' Gillian greeted him with a smile which was genuinely spontaneous and liberally dispensed for those she liked. He was clearly one of her favourites. At her own discretion she had long stopped formally addressing people with their title and was on first name terms not only with the junior scientists but also with senior consultants. This was one of Gillian's habits Catherine had frowned upon: to be over familiar was a manifestation of her thoroughly bad manners.

'The boss is already waiting for you.'

'Send him in. Better late than never,' beamed Blakemore from one of the screens as she announced Mark's arrival.

Blakemore's office was larger than Mark's and also faced north with the same panorama of London. It was an impersonal space, as if its inhabitant wished to keep his interests hidden from prying eyes. There were no pictures on the walls, no family photographs on the desk and no textbooks on the shelves. Blakemore was a short, rotund man with a barrel chest, which seemed to have continued imperceptibly into the lower half of the body without any allowance for a waist. The massive torso was carried by short muscular legs, and his arms were disproportionately long for his body. His pepper and salt hair was always cropped short, in striking contrast to his eyebrows, which sprouted uncontrolla-bly in all directions. On a superficial survey he looked more like a retired boxer than the director of one of the most prestigious neuroscience institutes in the world. This impression was imme-diately expelled when he started to speak.

A northerner by birth, he had qualified in medicine in Manchester and after a period of training in psychiatry at the Maudsley Hospital in London had returned to his native city. His scientific career fell outside the golden triangle of London-Cambridge-Oxford: he was the product of the Manchester Insti-tute of Science and Technology where he had been appointed to the chair of psychiatry at the age of thirty-nine.

He was brilliant at grasping complex problems and intuitively selecting the best solution among the alternatives. Yet there was an element of superficiality in the way he operated. 'Blakemore's superficiality runs deep,' his detractors quipped; indeed he worked with broad brushes and attention to detail was of little interest to him. Focusing on the minutiae of a project had fre-quently been left to one of his assistants.

Blakemore was relaxed. He had obviously enjoyed Cameron's seminar and his mood was buoyed by the anticipation of his dis-cussion with Mark. Chadwick was one of his most able scientists and Blakemore knew that he would go far. He envisaged Mark as being one of his potential successors, taking over the direc-torship of the Institute one day. The only item on the agenda for their working lunch was a chat about the programme grant to the Health Sciences Research Council – a vital source of funds on which Mark's future research depended.

'Come in and sit down,' said Blakemore, ushering Mark in. On the side table there was a plate of sandwiches but Mark turned down Blakemore's offer of refreshments. He had no appetite.

'Did you read the press release on your paper?' Despite Mark's protestations Blakemore had already arranged it for the next morning, clearly with the intention of creating as much public-ity as possible.

'Yes, I did – although I think we should have waited.' He could not hide the disapproval in his voice.

Blakemore fixed his gaze on him and asked sharply:

'Why?'

'After all, this is a hypothesis which we've yet to prove.' When Catherine had told him the date of the release, he was annoyed. Instinctively he shunned publicity, yet he had to accept that wider public knowledge of his work was in his interest. However, with Dufresne's visit on his mind, the *Nature* article lost its priority for the time being.

'Leave the publicity to me. It can't do any harm in getting your grant. And there is no doubt that it's crucial to obtain funding for your work. Without this programme grant you simply can't continue your research.'

As Mark sat down, Blakemore started to talk about Cameron's seminar but since his visitor did not respond, he suddenly stopped.

'Oh, you couldn't come, too busy with your experiments? How did they go?' Apart from Maria Lopes, Blakemore was the only scientist in the Institute who had known that he had been conducting the first preliminary test run earlier in the morning.

'They were fine – I think we're on the right track.' From the flatness of his voice, Blakemore realised that something was not right. Normally Mark would have burst in with the news, eager to share with him the success of the experiment. Intuitively, Blakemore perceived that the agenda of their meeting was going to change. He was not a man of many words and did not hesitate to wade in straight away.

'What's the matter?'

Mark waited a second or two while running over the sequence of events in his mind, before calmly giving an account of his encounter with Robert Dufresne. By the time he began speaking, he had overcome the initial emotional turmoil caused by his unexpected visitor. He saw the challenge facing him and this understanding enabled him to talk dispassionately. He felt detached, as if someone else had been involved. When he finished, there was a momentary silence.

Listening intently, Blakemore shifted his gaze from the view, resting it finally on Mark. He frowned and as his skin concertinaed into deep furrows, his eyebrows shot up, spiking the air. The room suddenly filled with a tense silence. Sitting motionless, he took a deep breath, like a diver resurfacing from the depth of the sea and stated the obvious:

'You have to make a difficult choice. It may affect your future career and indeed the future programmes of the Institute.'

Up until that moment Mark had been confident that Blakemore would stand behind him. However, the last sentence raised an alarm. Blakemore's concern with the future of the Institute was an entirely reasonable attitude for which he could not blame him; nonetheless he would be considerably more exposed if he lost this powerful ally.

'By the way, we should not underestimate Dufresne.'

'Do you know him?' asked Mark with surprise in his voice.

'Not directly. But a close friend of my wife works in the same department of Home Security. Some of their work is very hush-hush. But she knows Dufresne alright – in fact she was on his appointments' committee.' Sensing Mark's impatience, Blakemore continued without waiting for any encouragement:

'I remember she had dinner with us on the day Dufresne's appointment was announced. Of course, we were all interested in London's security supremo. Dufresne's meteoric rise to his current position – he's only thirty-eight, you know – wasn't a surprise to those who knew him. He was recruited at Warwick by one of his professors. Apparently he has a phenomenal memory both for facts and faces. It's rumoured that he suffers from a mild and rare variety of Asperger's but all the neuropsychological tests carried out returned an impeccably clean bill of psychological status and mental health.' Blakemore paused and looked at Mark:

'He also has a reputation for being utterly ruthless. We should

try to avoid a confrontation with Home Security. At all costs.'
This was a barely hidden warning to Mark.

'They are a very powerful bunch with influence over many
institutions in the country, supported by the Government. The
Health Sciences Research Council is no exception – unfortunately they aren't immune to the Government's meddling since
their budget is from the Exchequer. It has been a long time since
they could honestly claim to be independent of pressures from
the Cabinet Office. To defuse the situation, I suggest that as a
first step, we review Fiona Cartwright's case. After all, she was
your patient. One could argue that you were responsible for her
health but not for her actions – no one could foresee what she
was going to do. The initiative should come from us – it would
be a tactical error to wait until we are told to do so.'

Blakemore paused again. Mark shifted in his chair, helped
himself to a cup of coffee and waited in silence.

'I am, of course, prepared to review her case for you. However,
it is imperative to call for a second, independent opinion.' Before
Blakemore could continue, Mark intervened:

'I hope you don't think she didn't receive the right treatment?'

'Of course not. But we shouldn't forget that one of our patients
was involved in an attempt that could have ended in disaster
for the whole country. We must demonstrate beyond reasonable doubt that she received the right treatment, so there can't be
even the slightest whiff of medical negligence.'

'We all make mistakes, but on this occasion I don't think that
I did.'

Blakemore seemed almost not to hear.

'Am I right in saying that Dufresne offered you funding from
his own budget to pay for the experiments involving his so-
called criminal group? Did he also imply that he might put in
a good word or two with the Research Council for your programme?' When Mark nodded, he continued:

'He offered you funding, as a carrot, if you comply but of
course he also has the stick: he will try to block your programme

grant from the Research Council. I have yet to meet Dufresne personally, but from what I heard from our friend in Home Security, he isn't the sort of character who easily accepts a refusal. He has the power and he isn't going to hesitate to use it. We may end up facing a formidable enemy. You have to make your mind. Whichever way you decide it won't be easy. I'll try to give you as much backing as I can.'

Mark realised that this was the end of the appointment. He thanked Blakemore for his support and stood up. But as he was leaving the office, his boss called after him:

'After all that, we haven't discussed the application you plan to submit. Once you've cleared your head, we should concentrate on the project.'

'Yes, of course,' nodded Mark, but as he was leaving Blakemore's office they both knew that their priorities had drastically shifted since the morning.

Having closed the door of Gillian's office behind him and still numb from the discussion with Blakemore, he felt a sudden need to leave the building, to get out into the fresh autumn air. He felt deflated. The meeting with Blakemore was unsatisfactory – they hadn't even discussed the grant application. He wanted to share his thoughts. To whom could he talk? Yasmina was probably still busy. Anne? Daniel? Being a clinical neuroscientist himself, he would probably understand more than anybody else not only the personal but also the scientific aspect of his conundrum.

In the end, he decided not to return to his office, and from the corridor he called Catherine, telling her that he would have a half-hour walk in the nearby park. Catherine's surprise was palpable. Mark never left the office so early in the day.

Having crossed the traffic on Denmark Hill, he entered Ruskin Park, a refuge of tranquillity a few yards from the main block of King's College Hospital. The park was nearly deserted: on a bench a young woman was reading a book while, with her free hand on the handle of an old-fashioned pram, she was gently rocking a baby with absent-minded regularity. On a bench opposite her an old man had fallen asleep; his jaw dropped and as his head rolled back the sun glinted on the dentures in his open mouth.

On a path winding towards the depths of the park, a couple was brooding over their visit to the outpatient department: the result of the consultation must have been ominous since the woman was sobbing into a handkerchief while the man had put a protective arm around her shoulder. Freshly fallen leaves crumbled under their feet. A smartly dressed woman in high-heeled shoes had removed, with her rubber-gloved hands, the copious excrement her loose-bowelled fox terrier had deposited at the trunk of a tree. Several cameras, strategically placed, scanned the park.

Mark passed the bandstand and a forlorn portico that once must have been the façade of a Georgian building nearby, and found a bench in a quiet corner protected by freshly pruned hedges of box. The afternoon sun was warm and as he enjoyed the sunshine he emptied his mind and presently surrendered to the physical sensation of warmth.

It was a quarter to three. He had been in the park for nearly half an hour. He should be able to get hold of Yasmina now: he pressed a key on his hand PC – she was free and answered the call immediately. Hearing Mark, her voice expressed surprise, since they telephoned each other at work only in cases of emergency. Mark gave a brief, headline account of his day: starting with news of the attempt on the President's life, his tutorial with the students, the first successful experiment of thought modification and the visit from Dufresne.

He was surprised that Yasmina did not ask more questions. Her failure to sense the acute anguish he felt since Dufresne's visit disappointed him. He felt a distance between them: Yasmina had remained outside his turmoil.

As he ended the conversation, he spotted a previously hidden camera on a tree opposite his bench, focussing its frozen eye on him. He did not know whether it was sound sensitive or not, nor did he mind. In this case the information gathering was superfluous, since Dufresne already knew everything. There was nothing additional the camera might have picked up from their conversation. Although the temptation was great, he was too disciplined to offer an obscene gesture to the lens. He stood up and made his way out of the park and, crossing Denmark Hill, walked back to the Institute.

In her office Catherine was busy on the computer. As he entered, she looked up:

'How did the discussion with Professor Blakemore go?' She was not inquisitive but she did care about him, Mark knew. And she also wanted to plan her work. Depending on Blakemore's approval, Mark was going to write the programme grant application and it was her responsibility to organise everything else outside its scientific content: to collate the budget by finding out salaries from the Finance Department, ring manufacturers and chemical companies for the costs of equipments and reagents, make sure that the named collaborators provided their letters of support in time, get the Ethical Committee's approval and lastly to send the final version, signed by Mark, his collaborators and the officers of the Institute, to the Council. It had to be timed to reach the next meeting of the Neuroscience and Mental Health Board: missing the deadline could cause several months of delay. Catherine was proud that this had never happened on account of her organisation. She looked surprised by Mark's answer.

'We didn't plan the programme grant on this occasion.' As he uttered these words, he realised that he owed her an explanation: 'We talked about Dufresne's visit.' And before he had finished the sentence, he knew that he would tell Catherine what had happened this morning.

'Would you like to come into my office for a few minutes?' Catherine followed him, her face emotionless. She was standing in front of his desk and would not sit down until Mark invited her to do so.

'You should know about Dufresne since you may be involved

in the consequences. You're my secretary and it's better if you're in the picture from the beginning. There is no need to emphasise that this is a confidential matter – I know you will keep it as such.' Catherine nodded.

When Mark had finished, she simply said: 'I appreciate your confidence more than I can say. If I can be of any help, please let me know.' She did not ask what would have been the most obvious question: 'Dr Chadwick, what are you going to do?' since with this enquiry she would have trespassed his privacy.

As if reading her mind, Mark said, 'I don't know what I'm going to do,' and with a clumsy attempt to be light-hearted, he added: 'However, there is one thing I do know – I'm going to pack up early today.' When he closed the door of his office, he could not foresee that this sudden decision would trigger a chain of events beyond his control and with far-reaching consequences.

9

Mark arrived at his grandparents' house in Belgravia at four thirty. His journey hadn't taken long: the mid-afternoon traffic from the Institute was surprisingly light. After Dufresne's visit he felt an incomprehensible need to see his grandparents. He wanted to talk to someone who knew and understood him, and his grandfather was just the right person. As so many times in the past, Mark knew he could rely on his judgement, coloured but never clouded by the close bond between them.

James and Clarissa Chadwick had been living in a white stuccoed building in Eaton Place for nearly a decade, vacating Cambridge Place for Mark and his brother, Anthony, after their grandsons had finished their studies. Their flat was the best in the house with two bedrooms, a drawing room and dining room occupying the entire first floor.

The trees in front of the house stood motionless in the sunshine. A camera above the entrance door recorded his every move. He hesitated for a second, looked up to face the lens; the camera recognised him and the door automatically opened. At the top of the stairs in the half open door, Agnieta, the Chadwicks' housekeeper, a short woman in her mid-fifties, was already waiting for him. For Mark, she was no ordinary housekeeper but an integral part of his childhood, having been the source of fairy tales and creator of the best cakes he had ever tasted. His grandparents had known her for nearly thirty years, and she had been a young woman in her twenties when they interviewed her.

She had come from Poland with the first wave of Polish

immigrants soon after her country joined the European Union. Tempted by the opportunities, she had landed at Heathrow penniless with her husband, Jurek. Their plan was to earn some money and then to return to Poland where, with their modest savings, they could have bought a better life. Yet, as the years passed, they realised that this strange foreign country had become their home and they abandoned the idea of starting life anew in their native land.

Agnieta had an open face, dominated by pale blue eyes and framed with long blonde hair. Mark was very fond of her slight but charming accent with its Slavic lilt. James and Clarissa found her trustworthy and reliable and in return they counselled her on the many everyday problems immigrants had to face, from filling forms for the Inland Revenue to selecting schools for their children. Their support gave her confidence, and when she and Jurek decided to apply for British citizenship, James offered to be one of their sponsors. When, many years later, James and Clarissa moved to Belgravia, it was taken for granted that Agnieta would resume her responsibilities in the new household.

For Agnieta the Chadwicks were the embodiments of the old-fashioned English as they had been imagined in Eastern Europe, the type that by now was becoming extinct: elegant, cool, resilient and understated. They inhabited a different world from the brash bullyboys of the City for whom she cooked and whose conversation and entire life seemed to revolve around money.

As Mark approached, he could see that Agnieta's face was creased with worry. Mark hugged her but she did not return his embrace.

'Your grandmother had another fit last night. It's the third this week.' Agnieta said 'fit' but Mark knew that it was yet another bout of the hallucinations, with all their sinister implications, that he dreaded.

Mark found his grandparents in the drawing room. James was reading a book in an armchair by the window where he could still catch most of the afternoon light while Clarissa was asleep on the sofa, covered with a rug. Although in his eighties, James Chadwick looked much younger: his hair was white but still abundant and well groomed and his eyes had not lost their inquisitive look. Despite the fact that he had shunned exercise when younger, he preserved his erect posture and trim figure. He was wearing grey corduroy trousers with a navy blue cardigan over a white shirt. Mark had hardly ever seen his grandfather without a tie even at home, and today was no exception. When Mark had asked about this habit many years before, James had simply responded that he felt undressed without one.

'What happened?' asked Mark, lowering himself in the armchair opposite James's, which was usually reserved for Clarissa.

'She's had another hallucination,' answered James but he suddenly stopped, looking in the direction of his wife to make sure that she was asleep. 'Do you remember when you first realised that Clarissa had Parkinson's?'

'Yes, of course I do.'

James's call had come at the end of a particularly busy day. He had longed to go home after his last patient, but from his grandfather's tone he immediately sensed that there was something more to his unexpected dinner invitation. The rituals of the meal were ideal for observing his grandmother without intrusion. It had not taken Mark long to make up his mind. He had decided that Clarissa should be seen by one of his colleagues in the National Hospital for Neurology and Neurosurgery, in Queen Square.

'The disease is probably still in its initial phase,' he told his grandfather after he had explained his suspicions. I may be unduly pessimistic ...' his voice trailed off. 'Of course, this diagnosis is far from certain. Tomorrow I will call Joel Horowitz at Queen Square. I have known him for years – he's first class and specialises in movement disorders. Parkinson's disease is his particular forte. He's an international authority in the field.'

Suddenly he felt drained as all the pent-up energy of a hectic day had deserted his body. 'You'll talk to Grandee, won't you?'

Even in the face of the depressing news, James had not been able to suppress a smile as Mark referred to Clarissa as Grandee. Despite his and Clarissa's encouragement and invitation, their grandchildren had refused to call them by their Christian names. He was going to be Grand and Clarissa Grandee when they became, for all practical purposes, Mark's and Anthony's foster parents.

Presently, looking at the recumbent body of his grandmother, Mark was grateful to Horowitz for the care with which he had treated Clarissa over the years. Turning to James, he said:

'At least we were fortunate that at the beginning Grandee responded so well to the treatment. The dopamine did the trick and didn't even cause any side effects.' James remained silent. From day to day he had witnessed the progression of the disease despite a new cocktail of drugs: the increasing tremor, the shuffling gait and, what upset him more than anything else, the way Clarissa's face was losing its fluidity of expression. Her posture had gradually changed, too: her once erect bearing collapsed into a stoop, as if she wanted to escape into a smaller space.

As if reading James's mind, Mark continued:

'I know more than anybody else, except perhaps Agnieta, how difficult these years must have been for you.'

'With your help and having Agnieta around, I've managed. She really has become irreplaceable. She comes every day now. Since her husband died, she spends more time here than in her own home.'

'In a way, we're her family now.'

James suddenly changed the subject: 'With hindsight, do you think we were right in insisting that Clarissa have the stem cell transplant? I accept that it is regenerative medicine's greatest advance, but in Clarissa's case the beneficial effects didn't last long.'

'On balance, I think we were.' Mark remembered that at the time James had needed convincing. He objected to the idea that embryos with a potential for life were destroyed, until Mark explained that with the rapid progress of transplantation methodology, they had abandoned embryonal cells a long time ago. Instead, the patient's own skin cells were used and were transformed by genetic manipulation into primitive stem cells, which would proliferate to produce masses of similar cells. These could then be programmed to mature into various cell types needed within the body to repair damaged organs.

'You were doubtful at first, I know, and you were right to hesitate. But the cells survived. Not all but a lot of them, enough to produce dopamine – as the functional imaging and improvement in her movements showed.'

'Yes, I know. For a while I was delighted since I felt that I had regained the Clarissa I had lost to the disease years ago. Life returned and even if it wasn't the same as before, the whole atmosphere of the flat had changed. Until eight days ago when on Sunday evening Clarissa suffered her first visual hallucination. I'm sure Agnieta has already told you,' James continued, putting down his book after meticulously inserting a silver bookmark crowned with an owl. 'Clarissa had another hallucination last night, practically as soon as we sat down to dinner. She imagined that Horowitz was in the room and wanted to examine her. Fortunately, the whole episode didn't last long, but it was upsetting.'

It must have been, thought Mark; James had always tried to minimise the effects his wife's illness had on him.

'Unfortunately,' Mark faced his grandfather, 'these visual hallucinations are landmarks of a new phase in the progression of the disease. An escalation we couldn't foresee and for which we weren't prepared. Some patients with Parkinson's develop dementia and this is more intractable than Alzheimer's which for the last few years has been successfully treated and more recently, even prevented.' James nodded; he was aware of the implications.

'During the years of her deterioration I've learned to accept and live with her physical disability but the thought that Clarissa is losing her mind I find intolerable.'

'From time to time I feel terribly frustrated and get quite angry. We're now declaring to know everything, well nearly everything about the brain, yet I am utterly helpless. I might be able to claim that I can modify the way people think, but I can't do anything when help is most needed.'

'Mark, you're doing a great job. You do the best you can. No one can or should expect more. You included.'

The ominous deterioration of his grandmother's health served for a while as a diversion from his own problem, yet he could not suppress thoughts of Dufresne's visit for long.

'Mark, is there something troubling you? Since you've arrived I can't help feeling that something has upset you. I know you're concerned about your grandmother but there's something else, isn't there?' James asked.

Without hesitation Mark told the story of Dufresne's visit earlier in the day. When he had finished, he experienced a sudden relief bordering on elation. For a while James remained silent. Mark looked at him: his grandfather froze in his chair. His question was unexpected:

'By the way, what was your visitor's name?'

'Dufresne. Robert Dufresne. Why do you ask?' James looked perturbed. He hesitated for a second, as if he had not heard the answer, then he said:

'What an odd coincidence. It must be the same man.' Now it was Mark's turn to be surprised. 'Exactly a week ago, I received a call from Alastair Fitzgerald, an old colleague. You wouldn't know him – he was one of the juniors in Human Resources, currently head of the department.' Mark did not know Fitzgerald but was quite familiar with James's position as the Director of Human Resources of one of the large international oil companies.

'His call came as a complete surprise since I haven't heard

from him for years. After my retirement, we met once or twice a year, usually for a gossip but occasionally he asked my advice – after all he inherited the job I once had.' James paused to listen and nodded to confirm that Clarissa was asleep.

'We met the next day for lunch in his club in Pall Mall. After the usual introductory pleasantries, he came straight to the point. As part of extensive auditing, this year Home Security asked the company to review all disciplinary proceedings going back many years. In one of the old cases, apparently, I was the first port of call. When Fitzgerald reminded me I remembered the people involved. In a nutshell, a large contingent of oil from Saudi Arabia, through reassignments and intermediaries ended up in the wrong place. In Haifa Harbour.' Mark could not suppress a faint smile.

'Potentially, it could have been a major scandal. The case was referred to the Ministry of Trade and Industry. At the time we didn't have any doubt that the Government, while wanting to know who the culprits were, would do anything within its power not to upset the Saudis. The company came in for some criticism: we faced difficult times and I offered my resignation to the Chairman, but the Board turned it down. The affair was closed until last week when an officer from Home Security paid a visit to Fitzgerald. High ranking, apparently. Hard as nails but pleasant enough not to ruffle too many feathers. With a bit of an aura of cloak-and-dagger, according to Fitzgerald. Nonetheless, it is odd to dig up this case. These people don't do anything without a motive and somehow I suspect that it wasn't his last visit.' James paused. 'His name was Robert Dufresne.'

Mark listened in disbelief.

'What an extraordinary coincidence,' James concluded.

'Or perhaps not quite a coincidence,' Mark interjected. 'Our encounter wasn't entirely amicable.'

'Did he threaten you?'

'No, he didn't. At least not directly.'

There was a light noise from the direction of the sofa. Mark turned around and he saw his grandmother standing; her rug slipped down to the floor. She was completely motionless as if paralysed from head to toe, but within a second she became agitated. With the small hesitant steps of a sleepwalker, she was moving towards the window. Her vacant, non-seeing stare was filled with horror. She lifted her right arm, intent upon liberating it from the mangled sleeve of her cardigan.

'Oh, it is there,' she screamed, 'the building has collapsed and broken glass is scattered all over the road and the pavement, and fumes in the air. Why aren't the police coming? Where are the ambulances? Where are they? Where are they?' In her excitement she wavered and for a split second she seemed to have lost her balance.

They both rushed to her but before they could reach her, she collapsed on the floor. They lifted her up. Her body was motionless. The terror left her eyes: her stare was fixed somewhere far away where they could not follow her. Mark gently laid her on the sofa. Her pulse was regular. He looked for bruises but could not see any: the Persian carpet had absorbed the effect of the fall. For a moment he gathered both of her hands and enclosed them into the safety of the nest of his palms. Her hands felt like the broken carcass of a small bird. James covered her with the blanket and, rearranging the cushion under her head, he kissed her.

'Are you alright, dear?' he asked solicitously, but no answer was forthcoming. By now she had calmed down and was looking uncomprehendingly at her husband. James walked to the exact spot where a minute before his wife had been standing. The street below was quiet: a couple of diplomatic cars were parked on the opposite side and a black cab was disappearing round the corner towards Eaton Square. He moved away from the window and at the same moment they looked at each other in the sudden realisation that Clarissa's terrifying vision might have been the reflection of a distant image from the past: a tragedy which had fundamentally changed their lives.

10

On Thursday, 17 September 2020 at 5.27 p.m. during the evening rush hour a bomb had exploded in Selfridges on Oxford Street in central London. Two minutes later another blast had shattered Harrods in Knightsbridge, also crammed with shoppers. Between 5.30 p.m. and 6.18 p.m. four further detonations had followed in rapid succession, aimed at paralysing the transport system of the capital. Bombs in the underground stations of Oxford Circus, Earls Court, Waterloo and King's Cross had affected the entire network and brought instant chaos to the streets of London. An unexploded bomb had been found on the Eurostar, which left the terminus at St Pancras at 5.32 with a destination of Paris. The triggering mechanism, recovered later undamaged, had indicated that it should had gone off exactly at the time the train was entering the Channel Tunnel, thus causing maximum loss of life and, considering the type of explosive, serious damage, if not collapse of the tunnel.

London came to a complete standstill. The devastation was beyond the control of the emergency services. At the epicentre of explosions the scenes were infernal. The department stores suffered extensive structural damage: in Selfridges three floors in the western wing had collapsed, but the devastation in Harrods was the most serious. The explosion wrecked the central staircase and the collapse of the surrounding areas created a large crater that grew concentrically as the floors gradually caved in. Several smaller explosions shook the building as simultaneous fires broke out.

The conflagration spread so rapidly that the firemen had to withdraw after their initial onslaught, watching helplessly as the roof collapsed and the flagship of London department stores crumbled into a mountain of smouldering rubble.

Mark and Anthony were with their grandparents that afternoon. Their parents had gone shopping without them – to choose a present for Mark's birthday. The first he knew of the events was when he entered the room where his grandmother was watching television. He was struck by an extraordinary sight. Bathed in light from the standing lamp, Clarissa's face was contorted in anguish, as if all her strength, every muscle in her face, was concentrated on expelling an explosive scream which had been stifled by an unseen terror.

Her half-stretched arm, holding the coffee cup, appeared to be suspended between her mouth and the saucer on the table. Her whole body gave the impression of having been wound for action but all the pent-up energy seemed to have been frozen into immobility. The dead flickering light of the screen clashing with the warm glow emanating from the lamp made the scene even more terrifying: Mark had never seen her like this before.

Clarissa must be having a heart attack, thought Mark, but as he followed her gaze, the horror he saw on the screen hit him with full force. In a split second, his attention shifted from Clarissa to the television, and his hearing, which had been numbed, returned with frightening acuity. He couldn't move, but just stood in the half opened door. On the screen he recognised what looked like his mother's red coat. He knew it well. It was his favourite and he often used it to locate her in a crowd. But now it was crumpled and dirty. His mother was lying on the pavement on the screen in front of him.

The first newsflash had been broadcast a few minutes after the first blast. It simply stated that a large explosion had occurred in Selfridges in central London. Television crews had rushed to the scene of carnage but as the events unfolded and the subsequent explosions had been reported, even they could not reach their destination. The police gradually cordoned off large areas of central London. All evening performances of theatres, concerts, ballets and operas had been cancelled. All terminals at Heathrow airport were closed, and no flights could take off or land. Until further notice flights were temporarily suspended from Gatwick, Stansted and City airports.

Londoners, hardened by decades of terrorist activity in their city, first by Irish nationalists, then by Islamist extremists, watched the destruction on television with unbelieving eyes. The ambulances could not handle the emergency, and owners of private cars volunteered to drive the less seriously injured to hospitals. All accident and emergency departments in London were placed on alert but they soon became saturated as an endless stream of the seriously wounded and the dying arrived. For a long time no one knew the number of those who had perished. The estimates grew alarmingly as night descended: scores became hundreds and then thousands. The 8 o'clock news the next morning gave the first official figure at 1,748 dead and 2,412 seriously wounded. No one doubted that the final figure was going to be much larger as those buried under rubble and trapped in the underground were brought to the surface, dead or alive. The communiqué confirmed that rescue operations would continue for several days. For some people the explosions brought back memories of the terrorist attacks of 7 July 2005 but the scale of the present attack, being incomparably greater, reminded many of the destruction of the World Trade Centre in New York in 2001.

At first no one claimed responsibility for the atrocity, but a few minutes before 10 p.m., just in time for the main news bulletins, three organisations relayed messages to the BBC and local radio stations. Two were from well-known Islamist extremist organisations, but the third was from previously unheard of Northern Irish Protestant terrorists, the United Ulster Freedom Fighters.

Unification, at one time unimaginable but something that ordinary people now took for granted had unfortunately reactivated Irish terrorism and this time it was the Protestants who felt betrayed and had taken up arms against the British. The intelligence services had picked up some signs of renewed terrorist activity in Ireland but were unprepared for this outrage: the chances that the UUFF would be able to mount an attack on this scale on the mainland were considered to be remote. For years, resources of the intelligence services had been channelled to tackle Muslim terrorism. Indeed, according to the first analysis, one of the Islamist extremist organisations was most likely to be responsible. As the intelligence services, experts in terrorism and forensic scientists pooled their information during the following weeks and months before a final report was issued, a surprising fact emerged. All the explosions, although long-planned, carefully co-ordinated and meticulously executed, were of low technology. The terrorists walked into department stores, railway and underground stations and left their deathly cargo, which went unnoticed for long enough to be exploded by remote control.

On the outside Mark and Anthony's young lives returned to some sort of normality quite quickly. Their grandparents moved heaven and earth to make sure they were cared for. But the psychological trauma of losing your parents was more difficult to cure.

For a long time both children had recurring nightmares of the bombing. A child psychiatrist, recommended by the family's GP, had examined them and on his advice they had regular appointments with a psychologist specialising in childhood traumas.

Mark clearly remembered their visits to Dr Robinson's office in Great Ormond Street. At the beginning he had been frightened, then increasingly relaxed and in the end he was quite disappointed when his weekly sessions ended. As his apprehension had gradually melted away, he began to trust and even to like the middle-aged man who seemed to care about nothing else in the world but Mark's well-being. Many years later, as he recalled these visits, he became increasingly convinced that the seed of his determination to become a psychiatrist was sown during these sessions. Without the bombing, perhaps I would not have become a psychiatrist, he mused.

He became quite fond of Dr Robinson, but unfortunately the same couldn't be said for his speech therapist. Almost immediately after the trauma, Mark developed a slight stutter. Most of the time it was barely noticeable: only when he became excited did his speech turn embarrassing as he struggled to utter a word. Long sessions with the therapist during his early teens greatly improved, if not completely cured his speech defect. With determination he overcame this handicap to become a competent and confident speaker, giving scientific lectures at large international conferences without reading the text. Only those who knew him well could detect a slight hesitation, a short quavering before certain words at times of stress. A few people thought it was a nervous mannerism but most, including Yasmina, found it endearing.

11

Leaving his grandparents' flat, he felt drained and depressed. For a short time the memory of the tragic death of his parents overshadowed the anxiety over Clarissa's deterioration. A sense of impotence overwhelmed him. And now, on top of everything he had to deal with Dufresne's visit! He could not escape an upsetting thought that by accepting Dufresne's proposal he might help to alter the behaviour of society's most hardened criminals and fanatical terrorists, like those who killed his parents.

He was reluctant to go back to the empty house and today more than any other time he did not want to be alone. It was only half past five and he had at least an hour on his hands before Yasmina got home. On a sudden impulse he called Anne at the Old Bailey. The direct line was intercepted by an officious voice, asking him to identify himself and the nature of his business.

'Mark Chadwick. Judge Bennett's ex-husband. It's a private call.' He immediately saw the absurdity of the term: privacy shared by all those who had recorded the conversation.

'What a surprise,' Anne said when he was finally put through. She sounded genuinely pleased. 'What can I do for you?'

'Shall we have a drink after you finish work?' Mark volunteered. 'I'm free now – I left the Institute early today.'

'You sound as if you had nowhere to go. With a little time to kill, let's look in to see poor old Anne,' she said not without a touch of irony. 'Has something happened?' Not waiting for a reply, she continued: 'That would be fine. I have to complete a dictation but I will have finished within ten minutes. Why don't you come to the flat? I'll be home at six, at the latest.'

He arrived early, leaving himself a few minutes to walk

around Bedford Square. At the end of a sunny day the twilight lingered, reluctant to surrender to darkness, and the houses had not yet withdrawn into the shadows of evening. Office workers were leaving the buildings and visitors to the British Museum were taking shortcuts to the underground and buses of Tottenham Court Road. Cars had long been banished from the square and traffic restricted to Gower Street on the eastern side.

Mark never ceased to admire the harmony of Bedford Square: the stark beauty of Georgian houses symmetrically lining the four sides and a garden in the centre with century-old plane trees, surrounded by cast iron railings. The square was a statement of classical simplicity. Its self-confident splendour did not solicit flamboyant statements. Yesterday's storm had prematurely denuded many branches, and dead leaves swept up into small hillocks on the lawn were waiting to be carted away.

As he passed the Architectural Association where Anthony had studied, the street lights came alive. Too soon, he thought: their cold glare shattered the serenity of the twilight. As if responding to his objection, the illumination was gradually dimmed. Mark recalled that from the beginning of the month computer-controlled sensors regulated the intensity of lights in central London according to the number of pedestrians and the flow of traffic.

The block of flats in which Anne lived was just outside Bedford Square in a dogleg of a street leading to Great Russell Street. An Edwardian edifice on which the architects had let loose their imaginations, its abundance of decoration and unexpected lines could not have been more different from the austerity of the Georgian houses nearby.

Before he could press the bell, he heard a click. The door was unlocked and he heard Anne's voice: 'Please come in.' A camera was scanning the entrance. He blinked at the unexpected flash: he was not recognised.

Anne was already waiting for him in the half opened door. They kissed each other on the cheek and he followed her down the long corridor-like hall into the large living room. Although after their separation and divorce he had visited the flat on several occasions and more recently with Yasmina, he could not help feeling strange coming back to the place where he and Anne got to know each other before they moved to Cambridge Place following their marriage.

They both liked the flat and Anne had decided to keep it: under the management of an estate agent they had let it to long-term tenants. The apartment was spacious – the rooms were large with high ceilings and odd angles which added charm and interest.

'What would you like to drink?' asked Anne.

'I could do with a gin and tonic. Not too strong – I'm driving today.'

Mark looked out of the window. On a bench in front of the Architectural Association, in the soft penumbra of street light, a young couple was embracing, oblivious of the distant figure watching them from an illuminated window. He envied their youthful exuberance, and suddenly he felt old.

Anne returned from the kitchen holding a tray with two glasses, an ice bucket and a bottle of tonic water. From the drinks cabinet she produced a bottle of whisky and one of gin, and with the expertise of a barman she mixed the drink for Mark while pouring a generous measure of Scotch for herself. They settled with their glasses on the opposite ends of a large sofa. Mark surveyed the room.

The flat had been decorated in pale pastels: shades of stone, grey and off-white; soothing without being anaemic. Pictures on the walls and cushions on the sofas injected patches of colour. Between two windows, protected from sunshine, hung Anne's favourite picture and prize possession: a Signac watercolour of St Malo harbour shimmering on the pale grey wall.

'Do you remember,' said Mark, looking at the picture, 'the first time we saw the Signac?'

'Of course I do,' replied Anne with a smile.

Since Anne was, as Mark had discovered early during his courtship, quite a connoisseur of nineteenth- and twentieth-century paintings, they had frequently visited not only large exhibitions but also viewings of auction houses. On that particular occasion they had gone to a viewing of an impressionist and post-impressionist sale in one of the Mayfair auctioneers off Bond Street. In the centre of one of the rooms they had come across a small group of people.

An exquisitely dressed middle-aged Japanese couple were dividing their attention between a Van Gogh still life held by the white-gloved hands of two porters and a man in his late fifties, who must have been one of the auction house's directors, wearing a sharply elegant suit, bow tie and a pair of tasselled loafers. He was guiding the potential buyers through the picture, and as they stopped to admire a Cézanne landscape nearby, they could pick up fragments of his explanation: '… an unusual subject …'; '… the previous owner …'; '… the colours are not unlike …'

It was a still life with crabs estimated between six and seven million pounds. As they were leaving the room, Anne burst out, her cheeks becoming uncharacteristically flushed:

'This is one of those occasions when I really feel bolshie. Can you imagine? That prick in his smart suit will be richer by a million pounds from the proceeds of the sale of that picture? Painted by someone who apparently could sell only a single picture during his miserable existence! There is something fundamentally unjust in life!'

Only later, while looking at works on paper had Anne calmed down and found the Signac, which was love at first sight. She decided there and then to buy the watercolour. And it was during this visit to the auction house that Mark had finally made up his mind to marry Anne.

'I love this flat,' he said as if he were still one of the owners. Yet everything had changed since he had lived here. After they agreed to separate, Anne had, to his surprise, returned to Bedford Square but decided to have the whole interior redesigned. Apart from the walls everything had been taken out. The bathroom and the kitchen were completely refurbished and from an odd recess in one of the bedrooms a separate shower room was created. The wall-to-wall carpet had been ripped out and wooden parquet laid. In an attempt to turn over a new leaf Anne had discarded all the old furniture. The kitchen and the bathroom had all the latest gadgets: everything was computerised and voice sensitive; software programmes ensured that the bathwater of the desired temperature could not overflow, the milk could never over-boil and the steak was cooked to the required level of juiciness.

From where she was sitting Anne could command the intensity of the lighting and increase or decrease the temperature of the room to a tenth of a degree. It was only here that their taste had diverged. Mark preferred to keep technology at bay in his home, reluctantly making allowance in the bathrooms to yield to Yasmina's complaints about their archaic state. Yet, he had to accept that in Anne's flat, the twenty-first century technology did not collide with the ornate Edwardian architecture. It was a triumph of the young interior designer whom Anne had commissioned for the alterations.

'How are your neighbours?' he asked, lifting his glass. His question was a mixture of genuine curiosity and a manoeuvre to gain time before he told Anne the real reason for his visit.

'Nothing remarkable to report. They are all still around.' The block had attracted a set of eccentric characters: a couple of broadcasters who worked for the BBC; the wife who edited one of the women's radio programmes, while the husband with monotonous regularity churned out obscure novels weighed down by ponderous philosophising, praised by the critics but ignored by the public; the German software programmer who had a penchant for black women whom he regularly beat up, their screams echoing in the corridor; the elderly artist on the ground floor who painted still lifes in sleepy pastel colours reminiscent of Morandi and desolate street scenes completely devoid of human figures: London as a ghost town. But their favourite was Henry Salisbury, a small independent publisher and inveterate alcoholic whose anecdotes on the London literary scenes had entertained them on many of the chance encounters in the lift or at the occasional dinner they had been invited to at his flat. Sometimes, they found him late in the evening in a deep stupor in the entrance hall; on one occasion he must have fallen asleep in vertical position, propped up against the wall in one corner.

'In the case of Salisbury, he is alive just by a hair's breadth or rather by the last few surviving of his borrowed liver cells. He has managed to blast even his transplanted liver with alcohol.'

Talking about the neighbours had brought back memories of their life together in this flat. Mark had met Anne at a dinner party given by a fashionable West End solicitor whose wife was one of the neurologists in the hospital where Mark spent his final clinical year. In the reverberating supercilious repartee, Anne had immediately attracted Mark's attention with her quick wit and astute observations. At the end of the evening they had exchanged telephone numbers and a week later they had met again. Their courtship was an intellectual discovery as much as a sexual journey. Six months later they married. Mark was twenty-six and Anne six years his senior.

Mark's intention to marry Anne Bennett had taken the Chadwicks by surprise. While publicly they both supported him, Clarissa had reservations she dared to articulate only to James:

'She's six years older,' she said disapprovingly, 'it doesn't matter now but it might be a problem later. And that accent!' she added half jokingly, half seriously. Yet she could not help but admire Anne's intellect and successful professional life. James smiled at this snobbish remark, so untypical of Clarissa. He was pleased with Mark's choice, 'a breath of fresh air' he thought. Anthony's support was even more enthusiastic: 'In Anne,' he assured Mark, 'you had found a life-long companion.' Unfortunately, this was not quite the case.

The first problem arose two years after their marriage. Mark's wish to have children early in their marriage was resisted by Anne.

'To be away for one year is a long time. Your reputation is written in the sand – so you're only as good as your last case,' she had said.

'How's Clarissa?' Anne asked now, sipping Glenmorangie, her favourite malt.

'I've just visited them and she isn't well. She now hardly recognises anybody. It's most traumatic for James – it's incomprehensible that someone with whom you have spent sixty years of your life looks at you as if she had never seen you before.'

'It's a tragedy. Made worse by the fact that in her case, even I know, there's little one can do. At least Alzheimer's can be effectively treated. Do you remember Jeremy Vaughn, my head of chambers? His wife had a mutation for Alzheimer's but genetic manipulation prevented the disease. Isn't that marvellous? Who would have thought even a few years ago!' Anne stood up and poured more whisky into her glass. 'I can't explain the fact that Clarissa and I didn't get really close to each other until she had become ill,' she remarked.

Mark nodded. Over the years Anne witnessed Clarissa's deterioration with sympathy, as the distant woman preserved in an air of perfection suddenly became a patient in need of help. And as Clarissa's life was shrinking, Anne grew in stature. Soon she was cutting an elegant figure: her movements while making a speech were harmonious and after the wearing of wigs had been abolished she made a special effort to get her blonde hair immaculately coiffed. Her only potential disadvantage at court was being shorter than average. The distance between the two women disappeared and Anne had remained a regular, if not too frequent visitor to Belgravia even after her marriage to Mark had broken down. Anne continued:

'Before her illness we even exchanged Christmas presents with the formality of presenting diplomatic credentials. Without you we would never have met – the smart daughter of a West Country farmer, ex-Cheltenham Ladies' College and the girl from a Glasgow working-class family of six who had started her education in a Catholic convent school.'

'You exaggerate quite a bit,' Mark interjected over-emphatically. He was, in fact, acutely aware that his own childhood had been filled with privileges created by his grandparents to compensate for the loss of his parents. 'You must understand her! She longed for her first great-grandchild and our children would have been the climax of bringing me up. The final reward for the long years of devoting her life to her grandsons and a satisfactory closure of her responsibility. I also …' It was at the tip of his tongue to make a long-suppressed confession expanding on why he also had an especially strong desire to have children, but at the last second he pulled back and the sentence trailed into silence. Anne waited for Mark to spell out the real purpose of his visit, but his eyes were glued to the Signac.

Unexpectedly she changed the subject:

'How is Yasmina getting on with her research?' Mark, who by now was ready to talk about his encounter with Dufresne, was disappointed at this diversion.

'Very well, indeed. She has just engaged a bright PhD student on a project you are familiar with. Terrorism.'

'Yes, she invited me for lunch a couple of weeks ago to ask my advice. Like a schoolgirl she came well prepared with questions at the ready on the legal implications of a PhD thesis.' The tone of condescension was difficult to miss.

'You seem to have come a long way from intensely disliking Yasmina to giving advice on the project of her PhD student,' Mark said, regretting being confrontational.

'You are wrong and you always have been. I didn't intensely dislike Yasmina – our marriage was already on the rocks. Her appearance in your life was just a piece of additional cargo, which finally sank the boat. In a way, I admire her. She is a spoilt brat who has everything and who has become accustomed to having everything – youth, beauty and family money. And to cap it all, she is even bright.' Once again, Anne betrayed her deep anger at what had happened between her and Mark.

Mark had to admire her feisty argument and could not deny that Anne had not changed much. Soon after they had met he went to sit in the Visitors' Gallery in the Old Bailey one day and was impressed by her exact delivery. She avoided gratuitous aggression and refrained from scoring cheap points at the expense of her opponents. Her no-nonsense style earned her the rather dubious respect of some of the old-fashioned misogynist dinosaurs of the Bar, but it was not in evidence now. She was unable, in the personal sphere, to avoid showing her hurt. Yet, in court she was a formidable opponent and particularly excelled at mitigation. She had a genuine understanding of the problems of dispossessed people on the edge of society, an experience with which, according to her, not many advocates at the Bar had been burdened. It was also, perhaps, Mark had to admit, why she found Yasmina's success so difficult to bear.

He wondered whether Anne still had, despite her professional success and social status, vestiges of deep-seated white working-class resentment against those immigrants who, within a short time, were doing so much better than their own community. From past experience, he knew that Anne would fiercely deny it, should he dare to raise the subject.

'I'm grateful for your helping Yasmina,' he said lamely. Finishing the rest of his gin and tonic, he hesitated for a second: 'You haven't asked me why I called you at the Old Bailey and wanted to see you at such short notice. I have a problem at work.'

'I know. I've heard your story. Quite possibly from a somewhat different point of view from the one you are going to present to me.'

Mark looked at her with disbelief: 'It's impossible! How would you know? From whom?' Possible sources of information flashed through his mind. But before he could draw the final conclusion, Anne spoke:

'I received an urgent confidential memo from Robert Dufresne. It was waiting for me this afternoon after I rose in court. I could only open it with a special code a few minutes before you called.' For a minute Mark was speechless.

'I hadn't the faintest idea that you knew Dufresne. What the hell did he tell you?'

'I'll answer your first question first. I can't say that I know him – I've met him only a couple of times.' Anne hesitated for a second. She was telling the truth, but not the whole truth. Like so many people in the witness box with their trembling hands on the Bible, the Qur'an or on the Old Testament. 'He thinks that you *are* responsible for Fiona Cartwright's death.'

12

For a second, he could hardly believe his ears. He was aghast and felt defeated by Dufresne who seemed to have been one step ahead of him. He glanced around the softly illuminated room. Before going on he wanted to be sure of one thing:

'Anne, is this bloody flat bugged?'

'I don't know. I've never thought about it. I don't think that my private life is worth that much attention. Perhaps it is bugged. You know, I couldn't care less. I don't have anything to hide. Nor do I have many visitors.' She continued: 'I gave up dinner parties a long time ago. What can they record? Our conversation? We've nothing to hide that they don't already know.'

Mark decided to throw caution to the wind and asked point-blank: 'Where did you meet Dufresne?'

'Do you remember the committee convened by the Government in the wake of the State of Emergency – in happier times it would have been a Royal Commission but by then no one bothered with royalty? We were invited to assess the legal implications of increased anti-terrorist measures the Government wanted to legislate, including the introduction of compulsory personal databases to replace identity cards. I met Dufresne at one of the committee meetings – he was one of the liaison officers representing MI5. He was a smooth operator who usually got what he wanted.'

Including me, she thought, recalling their brief sexual encounter without contentment or shame. It had happened after the final session of their committee, not in one of the Whitehall ministerial conference rooms but in a country house, thirty-odd miles northwest of London. It had been at the party, celebrating the winding up of the committee after agreeing on the final set of recommendations when they both had drunk too much champagne. Dufresne's flirting, charming and not too pressing, had delivered her to his bedroom. After their brief but pleasurable lovemaking she could not wait to escape, yet she had felt no remorse. As they met next morning over breakfast chatting about how to get back to London, they had both been certain that the previous night's little adventure was not going to be repeated and was better forgotten.

Mark did remember the committee and his surprise, too, when his wife, not yet a KC, had been appointed to it. At the time he could not foresee that it was the committee that would finally seal the fate of their marriage.

'Do you remember the arguments we used to have when you came home late at night exhausted?'

'I would rather forget them. We were very foolish. I was in favour of the changes that were accepted in the end. You were bitterly opposed to them.'

'Yes, I was. I remember accusing you of trying to justify the wholesale surrender of our civil liberties. These were the recommendations which laid the foundation for, and sanctified the Surveillance State.'

Mark could still vividly recall those turbulent weeks when their discussions had been less good-natured than today's. When Anne returned late in the evenings from a session of the committee, their nightly arguments had become fiercer as he gradually found out the comprehensive nature of fundamental changes to be introduced. When Mark tackled Anne, she was far from apologetic. On the contrary. She claimed that it was not only possible but sometimes also desirable to restrict personal freedom in favour of the common good of society. And the time for such drastic changes had arrived. He was amazed that the free-spirited woman he had married only a few years earlier could be part of what he increasingly regarded as a conspiracy against personal freedom. He did not find Anne's acquiescence any more acceptable when he learned from her that there had been considerable pressure on each of the handpicked members of the committee.

'Where is the independence of the English judiciary?' he protested. He was shocked by Anne's cynical response.

'The independence of the judiciary? That went quite some time ago.' Anne had to confess that even the English legal system, whose powerful practitioners had a long and honourable tradition of defending their freedom, had not been immune to outside interference. Surrendering the principle of *habeas corpus*. Shifting the onus from prosecution to defence to exonerate the accused: guilty until proved innocent. The increasing power of the State Prosecution Service. Trials without juries. Manipulating the appointment of senior judges.

Holding by now an empty glass in his hand, Mark turned to Anne: 'Would you support the same recommendations now?' This time the answer was slow to come, but when it came it was definite, expelling any lingering doubt that Anne might have changed her views.

'Yes, I would.' Mark looked at her with incredulity.

'I honestly felt that we simply didn't have a choice. Something had to be done. For a long time a delicate balance had been maintained between civil liberties, personal freedom, human rights, call it whatever you like, on the one hand, and the security of the State on the other. If you think that civil rights are absolute, then of course, you are wrong.'

For a while Mark remained silent and then he said: 'I remember our arguments at the time when the State of Emergency was introduced, but I was young. It has taken Dufresne's visit today to force me to rethink my whole position. Until today I simply wanted to get on with my work, unhindered. After today this may not be possible anymore.'

Anne was visibly annoyed.

'Come on, Mark, don't exaggerate! If I understand correctly from both you and Dufresne, he asked you to run your experimental programme on some people who have been under investigation for criminal activity including prisoners who have already been convicted for terrorist activities perpetrated before the State of Emergency. I can't see the difference between his request and the work you've already been doing. Apart from anything, I would have thought you might want to avenge your parents,' she added brutally.

Mark was vehement: 'You must see the difference. With the thought modification programme, which is still in an experimental stage, we'll try to help patients with a variety of serious psychiatric conditions like depression, phobias and the like. We'll do this with the full consent of the patients after the whole procedure has been explained to them. We'll follow, letter by letter, the guidelines of the General Medical Council and also get the approval of the Ethical Committee at the Institute. It isn't sinister brainwashing by which we use patients to our own end or for the advantage of a third party. They seek help from us, and they'll be treated according to the best of our knowledge, for their own benefit.' Mark became more agitated:

'The request from Dufresne is totally different. He wants me to programme his detainees and prisoners to turn these so-called criminals, the terrorists and the enemies of the State, into law-abiding citizens. This is classical brainwashing, demanded by a third party and in the interest of a third party. Can't you see that by using psychiatry, or for that matter any other branch of medicine, as a sort of agent of security negates our humanistic tradition and moral conduct?'

Anne interrupted: 'But they would give written permission for the treatment.'

'Yes, that's Dufresne's line. Do you believe that they would agree of their own volition? Don't you think that Dufresne's boys would use threats, coercion and if necessary even torture?'

'Don't be ridiculous. No one is going to be tortured. We don't quite live in a banana republic yet. I think you should collaborate with Dufresne and I know that you'll regret it if you refuse him.'

He tried to control himself but burst out in anger: 'Is this a threat? You seem to be a willing partner to Dufresne's blackmail.'

'I'm not an accomplice to anything.' Anne raised her voice: 'This isn't blackmail. What Dufresne asked you to do is common sense.'

'Is it really? Would you convict an innocent man because somebody put pressure on you, insisting that the accused represented a potential danger to the State?'

Mark did not expect an answer. Yet, after a momentary silence Anne responded with firmness:

'Your example is clearly wide of the mark, and you know it. To convict an innocent man is always wrong – injustice can't ever be right. What Dufresne is asking you to do is to help people who are in need of your expertise.'

Mark retorted: 'The manipulation of others by duplicity destroys professional standards and undermines society.'

To Mark's amazement, an unexpected couple of bars of a Chopin waltz sounded and was followed by a mellifluous male baritone: 'Anne, it is half past seven. Time to change for dinner.'

'Sorry, this is *not* my new lover, only my latest gadget, reminding me of tonight's engagement.'

In the argument Mark did not notice how quickly time had passed.

'I must also go – Yasmina will be at home by now. Thank you for listening. Don't bother to see me out.'

'Mark, you *are* going to do it. Keep me informed.'

As Mark turned back from the hall, he caught a glimpse of Anne calling up a number. But he did not know that it was Dufresne's.

13

Mark stepped out into the deserted square. Only two members of the National Guard were peering into the garden in the centre, their powerful torches scanning the lawn and the bushes to make certain that no uninvited visitor might spend the night there. The central white stuccoed buildings, larger and grander than their brick neighbours were brought into sharp relief by the street lights. The cool air of the autumn evening sharpened his senses after the controlled ambience of Anne's flat. Their last exchange had upset him. He took deep breaths and quickened his steps as he walked towards his car.

Before starting the engine he suddenly remembered that he had switched off his micro-PC: he had not wanted to be disturbed during his visit to Anne. Two messages were waiting for him: one from Yasmina saying that she might be a little late and the other from Catherine asking him to call her whenever he picked up the message. Yet another unscheduled intrusion in one day annoyed him; from the tone of her voice he could tell that it was something important. At his command the micro-PC called Catherine.

'Dr Chadwick? Thank you for calling me back.' Catherine's perfect manner made Mark smile. 'I wouldn't have bothered you this afternoon but Professor Blakemore asked me to contact you. He has received a call from the Health Sciences Research Council. Professor Brierley, the Chairman of the Neuroscience and the Mental Health Board, has informed him that your grant application isn't going to be considered at their meeting this year, and will come up, at the earliest, in June.' Catherine stopped. She understood the disappointment Chadwick must have felt and wanted to console him but she only said: 'I'm so sorry.'

'Thank you, Catherine. See you tomorrow morning.'

He sat in the car unable to start the engine. The news was disappointing: not only a couple of months of work had been invested in the application but also the future direction of his entire research depended on its success. Could it be the hand of Dufresne? Anne's argument was ringing in his ears. It was not the first time that the Council had run out of funds but usually not halfway through the financial year. Yet, it was Brierley who had encouraged him earlier to submit the application by the deadline at the end of October.

Finally, he forced himself to start the engine. Despite the draconian regulations of reducing the number of cars in central London, the evening rush hour traffic had not yet abated. As he slowly turned into Tottenham Court Road, he joined stationary traffic. Roadworks further north, from the corner of Grafton Way extending up to University College Hospital, had closed off one of the lanes, causing a real jam. Traffic lights changed from red to green and then back again but the cars did not move. Stopping and starting, he barely made any progress. It took ten minutes to pass Goodge Street underground station, covering a distance of a couple of hundred yards.

At the end of a dreadful day Mark became increasingly impatient to get home. He tried to relax, but, locked in traffic, tension was growing in him. I must concentrate on the traffic, he warned himself; but he barely noticed the cars around him. Different thoughts were racing through his mind, clashing with each other, jostling for a solution. His visit to Anne had disappointed him. He expected, foolishly and without justification, that Anne would, dispassionately with her analytical intellect, serve up an easy answer to his dilemma. Or at least, take his side. Instead, he felt betrayed and defeated.

I must get out of here, he thought, and began to negotiate his way towards a left-hand filter to escape into Howland Street. He inched his way towards the filter but the cars already in the left-hand lane would not stop to allow him in. Being in the wrong lane and waiting to squeeze his car in, he had been holding the traffic up and the cars behind him started to hoot. Other drivers looked at him disapprovingly and he could see the angry face of the driver of the car that had just managed to get away from behind him mouthing, 'Idiot.'

He was upset at having attracted attention to himself and at the same time ashamed of being impatient. After a couple of minutes which seemed an eternity, one of the drivers, already in the filter lane, took pity on him, flashed his headlights and stopped, allowing him to get into the lane of escape. At that moment the filter turned green. He started to move into the gap. In his eagerness to flee the frustration of the jam and the unpleasant scene in which he had become the focus of other drivers' irritation, he turned the lock too hard and hit the bumper of the car in front of him.

For a second he could not believe his bad luck. He sat there numb without realising that his engine was still running before he regained his composure and turned the ignition off. This stupid, entirely unnecessary accident was waiting to happen this evening, the worst possible time at the end of a draining day. His home was so near, yet now it seemed beyond his reach: he would never get back into the protective cocoon of his house.

The other driver, a man in his mid-fifties wearing a suit and tie, got out of his car first. As Mark walked towards him, he glanced at the other car but he could not see any obvious damage.

'You should have been more careful,' said the man accusatorily but without any trace of belligerence. It was a statement in the full knowledge and safety of his right conduct: he was clearly above blame. Mark felt a sudden relief, realising that the formalities would ensue in a civilised manner without arguments and venomous recriminations. He nearly said 'Sorry, it was my fault', but at the last minute, remembering the insurance company's advice that under no circumstances should one accept responsibility in such cases, he refrained and just said:

'As far as I can see neither car has been damaged. I was coasting at barely four or five miles an hour, the impact was minimal and our airbags have not been activated.'

In Tottenham Court Road the traffic had ground to a complete standstill. A couple of drivers got out of their cars to identify the cause of the hold-up. The atmosphere had suddenly become edgy: frustrated commuters had been eager to escape to the peace of their suburban homes. Mark and the driver of the Pluton hurried back to their cars and pulled up further along on New Cavendish Street in the shadow of the Telecom Tower where there was a little more space in a parking lot for residents.

'If you switch on your headlights we could see the back bumper better,' suggested the driver of the other car but the brighter light revealed only a superficial scrape, not even a dent, right below the bumper, which would not require any body work; only the application of one of those paint restoring liquids whose effect is as good as the promise of their advertisement.

'I don't think we would need it but just in case, we should exchange contacts and our insurers' names,' said the driver. As he handed his business card to Mark, he sounded as if for him the incident had been closed.

Mark looked at the card: 'Dr Paul Morton, Senior Sales Executive,' it read, followed by the name of a large multinational pharmaceutical company. At that moment his phone rang. He looked at the screen: it was Yasmina. Although she tried to smile her face was sombre and she sounded worried.

'Where have you been? You're more than an hour late.' Yasmina was right to ask: it was five past eight.

'There is a traffic jam in Tottenham Court Road and I had to stop in New Cavendish Street.' He hesitated, unsure whether to tell her of the accident, but decided that this unpleasant news could wait until he got home. 'I'll be home in five minutes,' and ending the call he turned to Morton: 'I must go.'

When he opened the door of the house, Yasmina came to greet him; she must have watched him arriving from the first-floor window. Even before he could embrace and kiss her, she asked anxiously:

'Where on earth have you been? If you knew you were going to be late why didn't you call me?' For a few seconds he did not answer. Standing still, he held her closely in his embrace and he could feel the tension gradually draining out of her body.

'I had an accident. Nothing serious – no one was hurt, and neither car damaged. I will explain everything. But first I must have a shower. In the meantime why don't you open a bottle of red wine? We don't have anything to celebrate but I definitely need a drink.'

With a glass of wine in his hand, enjoying the presence of Yasmina and the security of his home, Mark was slowly beginning to unwind. In a calm voice he progressed through the afternoon and the early evening, hour by hour, starting with the unscheduled visit to his grandparents, Clarissa's hallucination, the visit to Anne, Catherine's call and finally the accident.

During his monologue Mark refilled his glass, while Yasmina had hardly touched hers. In the past he had frequently teased her that being a Muslim she was deep down a teetotaller who drank an occasional glass of wine only to keep him company. After Mark had finished, Yasmina remained silent for a minute, then she said:

'From your description Dufresne sounds like a formidable enemy whose path you cross at your own risk.' She lifted her glass, warming it in the palms of her hands and at the same time gently sloshing the wine around before taking another slip. 'Not a little apparatchik, not an anonymous cog in the machinery of the State, but a man of real power.'

As she spoke, he felt that suddenly a distance was growing between them and Yasmina's matter-of-fact style, echoing Anne's a couple of hours previously, unsettled him. He had not expected an outpouring of sympathy but he could hardly suppress a sense of disappointment. He said nothing. Reaching for the bottle, he poured another glass of wine. 'Your third,' noted Yasmina, not without a hint of disapproval.

'And whilst we're talking of Home Security, it's probably only an interesting coincidence. Nothing more, nothing less. You know Ted, don't you? My latest PhD student – a very bright boy. He was telling me that his college had been visited by Home Security recently to popularise the service. One of their regular PR exercises. And of course to spread the net for potential candidates later. He was much impressed by their speaker.'

'Did Ted tell you his name?'

'Yes, it was Dufresne. But as I've said it could be and probably is a coincidence.'

'Don't you think that there is at least one too many?' By now Mark was not even surprised at yet another unexpected appearance of Dufresne in his life. No need to be paranoid, he thought, as he realised that Dufresne was clearly pursuing him with determination, insinuating himself into every aspect of his life. Yasmina continued: 'And he wants you to program criminals and terrorists into law-abiding citizens. I could ask: and what is wrong with that?'

'Everything,' exploded Mark with anger he could no longer hide, 'and you know it.'

Yasmina did not flinch: 'Mark, don't be naïve. You know as much as I do that the State has been using scientific arguments for a long time for its own end. We are told what to eat and what to avoid. How much water to drink. To avoid obesity. To take exercise. The list is endless. Of course, all the hectoring is in our interest, they say. But not always. Digging into the archives by coincidence I came across a long defunct non-governmental organisation, and believe it or not they would decide which treatments or newly developed drugs could be given or prescribed within the National Health Service. Their independence, how shall we say, might have been somewhat curtailed by the fact that the purse strings were held by the Government. Problems arose when new drugs for the treatment of Alzheimer's disease or breast cancer weren't recommended for the simple reason that the beneficial effects didn't justify the financial costs.'

'That is an entirely different problem. There must have been an expert body whose advice the Government of the day sought.'

'Mark, what would you do if you could prevent a determined terrorist blowing up an airport terminal or a busy shop?'

Suddenly, he felt completely drained of his remaining power. A pleasant sensation of floating weightlessly in the room washed over him: the warm glow of the lights, the chimes of the carriage clock, the soothing effect of the wine drunk on an empty stomach. He wished to preserve these moments of calm but knew that this state of grace was only temporary and would be destroyed by the doubts of the night.

'I don't know. I haven't had a terrorist in my consulting room yet. Only a high-ranking officer of Home Security. And I find him more terrifying.'

14

Next morning, unfortunately, he was not allowed to take his car to central London and had to use public transport. He left his house early, but Catherine was already in her office.

'I am sorry I called you yesterday afternoon but I thought you wanted to hear the news from the Research Council.'

'You did absolutely the right thing.' Before he could reach his office, she called him back.

'By the way Professor Blakemore asked for you to see him at ten.'

On his desk he checked the screen: apart from this unscheduled appointment the morning was free until his clinic started at two o'clock. Sharp at ten o'clock, he knocked on the Director's door. Brushing formalities aside Blakemore had started even before he could sit down.

'Bad news. Certainly a setback. The Council contacted me yesterday afternoon. Apparently they've run out of money. This informal communication may not be the last word from them, but I have my doubts. We have no guarantee that they would support your programme in their June meeting.'

Meddling in his colleagues' professional life was not normally Blakemore's personal style, but he followed and discreetly supervised the progress of each of his senior staff. He paused, and then asked:

'Do you think that Dufresne might have played a role in the Council's decision? Of course your project isn't the only one being deferred, and they might genuinely be short of funds but they had assured us that this programme was a priority for them.'

Mark simply nodded his head in agreement, adding:

'It's too much of a coincidence.' He felt that Blakemore had not put all his cards on the table and was holding back some information. Neither was he sure whether Blakemore's question about Dufresne's interference was a mere formality to gauge his opinion or an introduction to a new revelation. But he was not left in suspense for long since his boss answered his own question.

'I don't know whether he or one of his minions took the trouble to talk to the Council but he did telephone me this morning.' Blakemore paused for effect, waiting for a response from Mark. This revelation was not a surprise: Mark was certain that Dufresne would try to exert further pressure on him through Blakemore. The only uncertainty was how the Director would react. Blakemore continued:

'He was polite to the point of finely honed diplomatic smoothness. He took considerable care to avoid the impression that they wanted to interfere with our work in any way – indeed they would be able to provide considerable support. Directly from the Research and Development budget of Home Security. I must admit that he had done his homework and was amazingly well briefed about our research.'

Mark could not help interjecting: 'Not surprising. By now Home Security must have scanned all our activities. As I am sure you know, they have access not only to our published work but they can also monitor our daily routines if they wish. They got a copy of the BBC documentary before its public screening. They probably intercepted our mail and bugged our conversations.' Blakemore chose to ignore this outburst, leaving Mark uncertain whether his silence was a sign of agreement or the reverse.

'Dufresne is very keen to get your approval to work on his cohort. He is convinced that everyone would benefit from this collaboration, not only us but above all the people under investigation and those who are already in prison. His persuasion was subtle and at this stage there were no threats. But I am under no illusion that our collaboration would make all the difference for you and for the Institute.'

The last sentence prompted Mark to ask the question that was unavoidable at some point during the meeting. 'Do you think we should collaborate with them?' Blakemore did not give his answer without consideration.

'On balance, I think, we should. Of course, on the condition that the patients give their permission to your treatment.'

'But they are not patients!' Mark objected, without realising that he had raised his voice. 'And even if they were, would their agreement be voluntary or obtained by coercion?'

Blakemore was in no mood to argue. He intended to draw the discussion to an end. 'I appreciate that this is a difficult decision. You've got time to think it over but let me know what you intend to do by the end of the week. If in the meantime you wish to come to have another chat, don't hesitate, just ring Gillian. Whatever decision you make we'll try to assist you.'

Mark stood up. For a second he hesitated and then asked, 'What would happen if I refused Dufresne's offer?' Blakemore was in no hurry to answer. Without looking up at Mark, he shuffled some files on his desk. Mark noticed with bemusement the nervous tic on his boss's face.

'I wouldn't, if you want my advice. I've somewhat changed my view since we talked yesterday, having considered Dufresne's offer very carefully. If you turn him down, we will have a serious problem in funding your research. If support from the Research Council isn't forthcoming, as indeed might be the case, we don't have a budget for your experimental programme. As you know, the costs involved are enormous – the Institute simply doesn't have the resources.' With every sentence Mark's despair increased. Blakemore paused.

'You can, of course, finish the preliminary screening, but after that cohort you have to stop until we obtain funds. It's as simple as that.' Blakemore stood up and walked towards him. Mark wanted to protest, but arguments had deserted him. They shook hands. 'Thank you' slipped out automatically and without looking back he left Blakemore's office.

As he walked back to his office, he replayed his dialogue with Blakemore. His attitude did not come as a surprise, for in Blakemore's position he might have had the same response. Putting the interests of the Institute as a whole before the career of a single colleague must be the right priority. Blakemore's support for him was clearly limited: he stood behind him only insofar as it did not jeopardise his overall plans. He could not accuse Blakemore of being duplicitous, yet he resented the fact that his boss, in his consideration, seemed to have ignored the fact that Dufresne's detainees and prisoners were not patients. They might have needed help but this they should have sought themselves and not have forced upon them.

Yet, despite his initial revulsion, Mark realised that he might not have a choice but to collaborate with Dufresne. Could he simply stand idly by while his whole research programme, the results of years of planning and preliminary work, was scuppered? Particularly now, after the first results were so promising. After all, he could help those people. Having left his card on Catherine's desk, Mark had Dufresne's private number and for a second he was tempted to call him.

In her office, Catherine was waiting for him with a message: 'Dr Chadwick, while you were with Professor Blakemore, you had a call from Paddington Green Police Station. Chief Inspector Templeton, Robin Templeton, would like to talk to you. He said it was a minor issue. Could you go to the station at two this afternoon and ask for him at reception.' Catherine looked puzzled but to reassure him she added: 'He was very courteous. He didn't volunteer what it was about and when I asked him he said that it was nothing serious. He gave his direct number.'

Perplexed by the news and wasting no time, Mark called the number. A recorded message informed him that Chief Inspector Templeton was not available until two o'clock in the afternoon. Suddenly a wave of anxiety gripped him. He went through possible reasons why the police might want to see him, with very little advance notice, in what was until a few years ago one of the

high security stations in London. Could it be the Fiona Cartwright affair? Or, more likely, could it just be about last evening's
accident? Was it anything to do with Dufresne? Was he getting
paranoid? He was also annoyed: yet another wasted afternoon.

He left the Institute a few minutes after one o'clock and resurfaced from the underground at Edgware Road with fifteen
minutes to spare. After midday, the rain had stopped but the cold
winds had not cleared the sky of a carpet of low-lying clouds. A
further downfall was in waiting: ready to drop any minute. Paddington Green was deserted. Only a few people made their way
hastily towards Marylebone Road: no one lingered on the paths.
The benches, which in good weather would have been occupied
by shop assistants and office workers snacking on sandwiches
and pre-packed salads in plastic boxes, were now deserted and
uninviting, covered with a film of slimy rainwater. Shaded by
ancient plane trees, the marble statue of a long-forgotten actress
looked forlornly at the stream of cars on the flyover.

Wandering around, Mark surveyed the Green. Once it must
have been a tranquil island but a flyover built in the late 1960s
had blighted it forever and now, high above, heavy traffic was
rumbling towards Oxford and beyond. The Georgian houses,
which had originally graced the Green, had long disappeared:
only a couple of brick buildings survived, reminders of a glori-
ous age of architecture in stark contrast with the drabness of
the council estate to the north. The offending tower block of
the police station, closing off the square to the east, dwarfed the
neighbouring buildings in its malign shadow.

He walked through the churchyard and stopped in front of
St Mary's church, looking up at its simple main façade facing
south. Unexpectedly its western door was open. For a second
Mark hesitated and then entered. From a table by the door, he
picked up a leaflet. The present church had been built at the end
of the eighteenth century on the site of two previously demolished predecessors, much altered in the nineteenth century and
restored to its original in the 1970s. He had passed this church

so many times, yet had never given even a fleeting thought to its architecture or history. He could not suppress a smile, thinking of how many harassed drivers on the flyover would know that John Donne preached in the first church and William Hogarth was married in the second.

There was no one inside. Someone had forgotten to switch the lights on, but the gloom of the interior was lifted by shafts of grey light filtering through the windows. The air was stale: a mixture of dampness, the smoke of candles and the lingering smell of dying flowers. A sensation so familiar to churchgoers was a new experience for him.

He could not remember the last time he had visited a church, let alone taken part in a service. For him, his grandparents' polite and restrained Anglicanism was a guide to decent behaviour and to a set of moral standards rather than a shining beacon on a path to unquestioning belief in a superior being. Unpredictably, Clarissa's saying leapt to his mind about how the good old C of E, while hesitantly groping for God, had always and unfailingly managed to stray into a social minefield.

A self-declared and rather belligerent atheist for a first wife and, currently a Muslim partner were not an ideal schooling in search of a Christian God, even if he had ever wanted to find one. In his life religion was not an issue and God had never surfaced in his thoughts. Not until now.

In this church he was a sightseer to satisfy his curiosity rather than a believer who came to seek solace. Yet the tensions of the outside world fell away the minute he entered. The church was deserted. As he slowly walked towards the altar, he could see the outline of a figure bent over the pulpit. Hearing Mark's footsteps, the man climbed down the few steps and walked towards him. He was in his early sixties with a mane of white hair. Wearing a thick tweed jacket, Mark spotted the dog collar peeping out beneath the loosely wrapped scarf.

'Good afternoon,' the man said, 'can I help you?' For a few seconds Mark was lost for words. He was taken by surprise, unaware of the priest's presence. The other man must have seen him from the moment he entered the church, and Mark resented the fact that unknown to him someone had shared his solitude. Yet he sensed that the question posed had not been an automatic, polite expression of formality, and the man in the worn tweed jacket would try to assist anybody in need of help.

'Thank you. I've just come in …' he hesitated, unable to define the purpose of his visit since the idea that he might have come to pray did not occur to him, and then finishing the sentence '… to think.' At the last second he had changed his mind, since he had wanted to say 'because I had a few minutes to spare before an appointment', but on an impulse which he could not explain even later, he had altered the second half of the sentence, but not just to be polite: clergymen were, after all, accustomed to visitors whose motives were sometimes far from religious. The priest's response surprised him:

'It's a good way to start.' For a second he contemplated the meaning of this short enigmatic phrase, but the priest did not elaborate any further. Mark remained silent. He looked at his watch. It was two minutes to two o'clock. I'll be late, he thought and, saying goodbye to the priest, he hurried out of the church.

The rain had started: a fine drizzle, which by the time he reached the police station had turned into a heavy shower. In the downpour the solid block of the police station looked even more drab than usual. It was a familiar sight from speeding cars, yet standing on the steps leading up to the main entrance and facing the flyover he gained a new perspective looking at the concrete pylons supporting the elevated road. Until 2036 Paddington Green was the high security police station in central London: the port of entry for high profile criminals into the labyrinth of the English legal system. Terrorists, home grown and foreign, murderers and armed robbers had landed on its threshold.

Its reputation as a high security station had suffered a major setback on a rainy November afternoon in 2032. In the rush hour, when the flyover was choked with cars and traffic became nearly stationary, terrorists had fired a handheld rocket from a passing car into the building. No one was killed inside and the damage was limited to one floor. The attempt had been a desperate act, as investigations had later revealed, of protest against the arrest of a group of alleged terrorists. Before police cars could get anywhere near the terrorists' car, they had blown themselves up. A film recovered from the flat of one of the terrorists had proved beyond reasonable doubt that the attempt to blow up the station had been a suicide mission: they must have known that in the dense traffic there was not the slightest chance of getting away. Apart from the driver and one of the passengers, four other people had died and a dozen more had been seriously injured. The police station had remained open while the damage to the building was being repaired, but the flyover was closed for two months, causing severe congestion in Marylebone Road and beyond.

One year after the State of Emergency had been declared a decision was made, within the framework of the reorganisation of the Metropolitan Police, to build a modern high security police station next to the already existing high security Belmarsh prison in east London. The move was most unpopular with lawyers who now had to trek to the Thames Estuary to visit their clients, but their vocal protests against the transfer had been ignored.

Immediately on entering, Mark was stopped and his identity checked. He was instructed to walk through a whole body scanner capable of detecting not only weapons and other metal objects but also explosives and drugs. At the reception a young police officer was on duty. Mark asked for Chief Inspector Robin Templeton. The duty officer screened the monitors:

'Chief Inspector Templeton is still busy on another case but he will be with you soon. I'll ask one of my colleagues to take you up to the interviewing room.' He pressed a button and from the door behind his desk another police officer emerged.

'Could you take Dr Chadwick up to interview room 35?'

Mark followed the officer to the lift. 'This way,' he said, pointing to the right as the lift door opened and they entered the corridor. They stopped in front of the last door. From the window at the end of the corridor he could see Paddington Green. In the rain, St Mary's was sheltering under the umbrella of trees.

The interviewing room was a small windowless cube with whitewashed walls and a bank of ceiling lights. In the centre stood a table with two chairs, one on either side. A jug of water with two glasses had been placed in the middle of the tabletop. The officer pointed to the chair nearest to the door:

'Please take a seat. Chief Inspector Templeton shouldn't be long.' The officer withdrew, closing the door behind him. Assured that he would not have long to wait, Mark sat down and surveyed the room. It did not require much time. Along one wall four additional chairs had been stacked. The lights were unremittingly bright. Four cameras mounted on the wall covered all aspects of the room. A glass panel ran the entire length of the wall opposite him. He could not see what lay behind it, but he was certain that this was the vantage point from which interrogations were witnessed, unseen.

He looked at his watch. It was two fifteen. There was nothing to do but wait. He stood up and walked around the table a couple of times and then he sat down again. He lifted the jug and poured water into one of the glasses. The water was lukewarm and tasted stale. He nearly spat it out but forced himself to swallow the first gulp, then replaced the glass on the tray. Hardly had he finished the move when a policewoman entered, bearing a tray with an identical jug and two glasses.

'Sorry, sir. We forgot to change the water,' she said breezily and was gone.

At two thirty the door opened and a stocky man in his early forties entered the room.

'I am Robin Templeton. Sorry for being late but a previous interview took much longer than expected. They should have given you something to read.' He shook Mark's hand and sat down opposite him. He did not wait for Mark to introduce himself. Nor did he ask for any personal details: Templeton must have checked his file on the National Database.

'You must be wondering why we asked you to come to see us.'

'Yes, I certainly am.'

'We would like to clear up a couple of loose ends concerning the accident you had last night.'

For a second Mark measured Templeton up as if he had not heard him and nearly cried out 'What accident', but he responded calmly:

'You mean the so-called accident off Tottenham Court Road? Actually, it was an *incident* – I bumped into a car in what was practically stationary traffic. No one was hurt and neither car was damaged. The third party didn't have any intention of making a claim, and in fact there weren't any grounds for doing so.'

'How do you know that the other driver didn't report to us or to his insurance company?'

'Of course I don't know for sure, but we seemed to have parted on amicable terms.'

'That's hardly proof. He might have changed his mind. Anyway, people often say one thing and do something completely different.' Even if he had previously had any doubt, at this point Mark realised that Templeton might have an agenda other than the accident.

'By the way, why didn't you report the accident to the police?'

'I thought that there was no obligation to report the accident if neither party suffered injury and neither car was damaged.'

'That was the law until recently, but we have introduced a "zero tolerance" on the road. According to the new legislation all accidents, irrespective of consequences, have to be reported to the police. Including those in which injury or damage doesn't occur. Even if neither party has any intention of contacting their insurance company.'

Mark listened with increasing incredulity since this new legislation did not make sense. Amongst the mushrooming laws pushed through a compliant Parliament by the Government, this one might have escaped his attention. But confessing ignorance might not count as a mitigating circumstance. Templeton continued:

'We also received complaints from other drivers concerning your conduct on Tottenham Court Road. They alleged that your aggressive manoeuvring to force your way into the filter lane immediately before the accident not only held up traffic, but was also liable to cause an accident. In our books this qualifies as dangerous driving.'

Mark wanted to ask him whether the other drivers really volunteered their complaints or whether they were contacted by the police, but he remained silent. Templeton, having now scored a point, relaxed. He pushed his chair back from the table and crossed his legs.

'Do you deny these allegations?' His tone had changed and the narrative had turned into questioning. Before Mark could respond, he continued: 'Would you like to see the evidence?' He pressed a key and on the right-hand side wall a film started to roll. In the traffic jam on Tottenham Court Road Mark recognised his car. From several cameras the images had been edited into a seamless flow: inching his way towards the filter lane in his attempt to escape to Howland Street, the obstruction his car had caused, the frenzied hooting of frustrated drivers and finally the collision of the two cars. Templeton froze the frame, capturing the moment Mark had begun to walk towards Morton and their encounter: two motionless figures in the light of a street lamp.

Mark watched the film with growing unease. He regretted the way he had forced his way into the filter lane but at the same time he was concerned about the malice Templeton had injected into the interview.

'The evidence we have,' Templeton said with hardly disguised satisfaction, 'clearly shows that you were driving without due care and attention. Your aggressive behaviour caused the accident.'

'I don't think that my driving can be described as dangerous. The collision between the two cars did not result in any damage. The other driver agreed that there was no need for either of us to inform our respective insurance companies.'

'Did he? How do you know that the other driver wasn't going to report to his insurance company?' Templeton asked again, more emphatically. 'This morning we contacted Paul Morton to get a couple of pieces of missing information. Just in case. He firmly stated that you had caused the accident. In a more thorough examination of his car in daylight, he found his back bumper dented. It might have to be changed. He's going to inform his insurer, so better if you do the same.'

Mark looked at Templeton with incredulity.

'I am surprised. Why did he change his mind?'

'Perhaps you should ask him that question. But I'm sure you agree that we should record this incident on your Personal Identity Database. We'll only issue an informal warning and endorse your driving licence. That's all. Before we do this we should record the events leading up to the accident. From the time you left the Institute.'

That his licence was going to be endorsed did not surprise him by now. Morton's deserting his original stance had prepared the way for the forces of law and order to step in. But why would Morton have changed his story overnight? Mark could hardly disguise his annoyance and frustration.

'I've nothing against running through the events of yesterday afternoon and evening. Although I'm sure you already know everything.' He said it with a touch of irony that Templeton elected to ignore. To recall his visits and encounters could not have been easier: he did not need to stop in the story from the moment he left the Institute to cross into Ruskin Park to the moment he arrived home to be met by a worrying Yasmina. As he spoke, his words simultaneously appeared on the screen. He formed his sentences with a scientist's precision as the computer allowed an uninterrupted flow. No corrections were inserted.

Templeton interjected only once: 'How often do you visit your ex-wife?' The question was impertinent and superfluous to the interview. 'As often as I wish to see her,' almost slipped out of his mouth, but he wanted to avoid a confrontation:

'Not very often – I usually visit her with Yasmina, my partner. Last night I went to see her on my own to discuss a personal problem.' Mark paused for Templeton to ask about the nature of his personal problem, but he did not take the bait and he finished without any further interruption.

'You've been warned and your licence has been endorsed. Although this is going to be recorded on your Personal Identity Database,' Templeton emphasised again, 'there are no consequences for the time being. However, you should drive more carefully in the future to avoid any further traffic offences. You don't want to be disqualified from driving, do you?'

This is the right note to end the interview, Mark thought, getting ready to leave. Templeton's next move caught him completely unawares. The police officer casually looked at the screen in front of him again and then, fixing his stare on Mark, asked:

'Do you know a woman who goes by the name of Julia Ames?' Frozen to his chair, for a second Mark could not speak. Yes, he did know Julia Ames.

They had met at medical school. It was in the cafeteria of the swimming pool of the Students' Union where Mark had got to know her. With her dark brown hair and deep-set brown eyes, sensual lips and well-proportioned swimmer's body she was one of the most attractive girls around. They became friends and then lovers. For him, despite a handful of short-term sexual encounters, she was the first serious love affair and Mark was amazed to find out that Julia, at the age of nineteen, was still a virgin. They had been together for nearly a year when Julia became pregnant. Despite taking all the necessary precautions, they were not prepared for this complication. To make matters worse it all happened at a difficult time, just before examinations. Julia was shattered.

When Mark suggested that she have an abortion, she flatly refused. As a Catholic her religion meant more than ticking the right box in the census. The only alternative was to get married but at twenty-one, in the middle of his medical studies, Mark was unprepared for family life. First, he confided in Anthony who laughed at him for even considering marriage. Finally, he consulted James. His grandfather reassured him of his support in whatever he chose, even promising to release his share of his parents' estate to help bring up the child. Yet, he also felt that Mark should not marry.

In the end Julia agreed to an abortion. She declined to accept the flowers Mark brought her after the operation. She skipped her exams and dropped out of medical school altogether. Their affair was over. Afterwards Mark felt guilty for a long time, but Julia Ames had disappeared from his life. Until today.

He pulled himself together: 'Yes, I did know Julia Ames. She was my girlfriend many years ago when I was a medical student.' He decided to attack, 'What has she got to do with the accident you're investigating?'

'To tell you the truth – absolutely nothing,' answered Templeton with disarming indifference. 'By the way, do you want to know what Julia Ames had been doing until recently?' Before waiting for a response, he answered his own question with barely concealed glee: 'She was supervising casual workers who fill up supermarket shelves in Lancaster. Would you like to see her?' And before Mark could say anything, the clip of a middle-aged woman, replenishing large boxes of washing powder on the shelves of a busy supermarket, started to roll. It can't be, Mark thought. Yet in the worn bitter face he could just discern the ruins of Julia's features.

'Where is she now?' asked Mark with barely concealed eagerness. Templeton took his time to answer. And when he did, he spoke with unnatural slowness, dragging out each word separately:

'This ... clip ... was ... made ... in Lancaster ... last ... year.' Mark was uncertain whether his adversary was playing for theatrical effect or was running out of breath at the beginning of an asthmatic attack.

'Is she still there?'

'No, she isn't.' Templeton was clearly not in a hurry to satisfy Mark's increasing impatience.

'Where is she now? Can't you tell me straight away?'

'She's dead. She committed suicide.' For a second Mark hoped that he had misunderstood Templeton. As the words finally sank in he felt sick.

'How? How did she die?'

'Does it matter? But if you want to know, she took a good handful of sleeping tablets and washed them down with a bottle of whisky. A clean way to go.'

Mark felt an irresistible urge to smash in Templeton's face but he remained nailed to his chair. Templeton stood up.

'Good afternoon, Dr Chadwick.' They did not shake hands. 'I'll send someone to escort you out of the building. It won't be long.'

After the officer had left the room, Mark remained standing: stunned, he could not easily regain his composure. He was devastated. He was unable to collect his thoughts: the confrontation with memories of Julia was as shocking as it was unexpected. He was completely powerless. Helplessness and shame only increased his rage. He felt humiliated. And guilty.

Mark was desperate to leave the suffocating room poisoned with Julia's memory. It was a quarter past three; he could hardly believe that he had spent just over an hour in the interviewing room: it seemed infinitely longer. He had no doubt that apart from the cameras in the room, he was being watched from behind the glass screen. The same policeman who had ushered him in before the interview entered the room a couple of minutes later.

Leaving the police station, he became aware of the outside

world: pedestrians hurrying to reach the safety of the pavement before the traffic lights changed to red, the flow of cars on the flyover, the maroon-tiled entry of the underground disgorging dishevelled passengers, the marionette figures in the glass office blocks, the lush displays of the Middle Eastern greengrocers. The church in Paddington Green beckoned and he experienced an inexplicable pull. For a second he hesitated but then he started off in the direction of Baker Street.

15

The rain had stopped. An easterly wind had thinned the clouds but the sky remained grey with the threat of more rain. As he walked along Marylebone Road he felt rudderless and depressed. The shock of hearing news of Julia after so many years stirred up memories he had hoped to forget.

The feeling of guilt returned with renewed force and he had to face the fact: he had ruined Julia's life. She had opted out of medical school for good and never continued her studies. Instead of having the busy professional life of a physician, she had been doing a soul-destroying manual job. The girl who did not want to have an abortion had committed suicide.

He wanted to call Yasmina but immediately gave up the idea: how could he talk about Julia on the telephone? From this disturbing thought, he forced himself to turn his attention to Morton – he must find out why he had changed his mind. Unfortunately Morton was not available. Mark left a message, asking him to call him back as soon as possible.

His afternoon had been broken and he did not see much point in returning to the Institute, since by travelling back and forth he would lose well over an hour. He decided to spend the rest of the afternoon in the library of the Royal Society of Medicine: an ideal place to recover over a cup of coffee and to look up some archival references in the original not available anywhere else.

He passed the meandering queue in front of Madame Tussaud's and crossed the road at Marylebone Parish Church. His footsteps echoed on the cobbled stones of the church courtyard: a shortcut between the main road and the High Street. The place was now deserted save for a solitary figure sitting on one of the wet benches. As Mark approached, the man stood up and in a barely audible voice asked for money. Mark passed him without saying a word but then suddenly changed his mind, turned back and fished a couple of coins from his pocket. It was an unexpected encounter: since London's clean-up operation began begging was an offence.

Marylebone High Street was full of shoppers. The temptation to stop for a coffee was great and for a minute he hesitated but continued his walk. He passed Wigmore Hall and entered the Royal Society of Medicine. The marble foyer of the conference centre was bustling with people. The electronic programme board advertised a symposium on immunology, sponsored by one of the large pharmaceutical companies. It must have been tea break since participants were leaving the main lecture theatre in droves to make their way to the glass-roofed conservatory. Waiters wearing old-fashioned black bow ties and white shirts were serving tea and coffee from large glistening urns.

After the ordeal in the police station, Mark felt at home. His anxiety dissolved; he submerged himself in the comfort of the familiar professional milieu – stimulating and competitive and yet reassuring and morale-boosting. They all spoke a common language: men and women of all ages, races and creed; working in hospitals or in research institutes, treating patients or working out molecular details of the human body, operating, or designing drugs. They all had a common purpose in their working life: to help their fellow human beings. To belong was a privilege and a responsibility at the same time, and he took strength from the fact that he was one of them.

Despite the increasing interference with the independence of the profession, Mark never regretted that he had become a doctor. Even before finishing school, he had made up his mind and recalled the event that swerved his course. As a pupil he had excelled in Mandarin, and Chinese culture and civilisation caught his imagination. His Headmaster encouraged him, raising the possibility of a fellowship to study in China. After university, this might open up a diplomatic career in the Far East, he suggested to Mark, with the centre of gravity in Britain's international relationship shifting towards China.

Mark was receptive to this idea until, during a history class, one of the boys, Theo Clayton, had suffered an epileptic fit. While the students looked on helplessly, terrified at the sight of the convulsed body, Miss Rogers, the history teacher had called an ambulance. After a few minutes Theo sat up, dazed, not remembering anything that had happened, but when Mark telephoned him in the evening his mother told him that Theo had been admitted to hospital. The next day he was diagnosed with a brain tumour.

It had been during the first visit to the neurosurgical ward that Mark had made up his mind. He was impressed by the urgency of the atmosphere, the purpose with which doctors and nurses seemed to pursue their duties and by the trust his friend and other patients invested in those who looked after them. In his gap year he volunteered to help as an ancillary worker in the London Hospital in Whitechapel. With his final results at school, he was offered a place at University College London.

During his clinical studies he soon discovered that of all the parts of the body, the brain was of particular interest. The complexity of the organ was daunting yet fascinating, and progressive discoveries of how circuitries of nerve cells function were about to lead to the understanding of fundamental mechanisms of neurological and psychiatric diseases. After qualifying, he spent two years in neurology jobs before embarking on training in psychiatry. He was certain, even after so many years, that in this final decision the memory of his childhood visits to the office of Dr Robinson in Great Ormond Street Hospital was instrumental.

As Mark was crossing the hall of the Royal Society of Medicine to take the lift to the library, he saw, disappearing towards the cloakroom, his old friend, Daniel Weisz. It would have been difficult to miss Daniel. At well over six feet he was taller than most people milling around the foyer and his mane of wavy red hair was unmistakable. His white skin was peppered with freckles, as if a pointillist painter had indulged in the use of brown pigment. Unusually for his complexion he had dark brown eyes, full lips and high cheekbones. Those who did not know him well had often been misled by the structure of his cheekbones, thinking that he was of Slav origin; in fact both his great-grandparents were Hungarians. Penniless, they had arrived in England at the beginning of 1957 after the Soviet invasion of Hungary following the revolution in October of the previous year.

Mark had met Daniel when they were in their mid-twenties. They had both registered for a symposium of the Association of Clinical Neuroscientists held in Wye, near Ashford in Kent. At the end of the first day after dinner Mark had set out for a walk, for unlike most of his colleagues he was not fond of late drinking sessions. The last glass of port at dinner satisfied all he needed and for him the social part of the day had come to a close. However stimulating his colleagues' company, after sharing the whole day with other people, he longed for solitude. He would have preferred to withdraw to his room to read, but he set out for an evening stroll instead, to clear his head after a day of lectures, seminars and workshops.

He walked through the dark Village Green in the direction of the river. He avoided the noisy pub on the bank of the Stour, crossed the old stone bridge and followed a narrow path along the river, leaving the street lights behind him. Liberated from the noise and pollution of London, he breathed in the smell of freshly harvested fields. The water reflected a full moon in the cloudless sky. He stopped suddenly: a few yards ahead of him, a lonely still figure stood on the bank of the river. For a minute he hesitated, not knowing what to do next, since it was difficult to bypass the silhouette on the narrow path without speaking.

'Hi. Are you from the college?'

'Yes. Daniel Weisz.'

'Mark Chadwick.'

'It's a divine evening. Too early to go to bed, but I didn't feel like joining the drinkers.'

Together they walked back towards the campus but neither of them wanted to go inside to bring the evening to a close. It was one of those balmy nights, a rare gift of English summers, when the temptation to stay in the open air until sunrise is overwhelming. They circled the Green several times before settling on a bench in the churchyard. Finding common interests came naturally. They gossiped about their teachers, some well-known professors, the excitement of new discoveries in neuroscience and the difficulties of getting a job in academic medicine in London.

'We should go,' proposed Mark looking up at the clock in the sturdy tower behind them, 'it's nearly one o'clock.' This evening encounter was the beginning of their friendship.

'What are you doing here?' asked Mark.

'I'm working in the library for the rest of the afternoon. I'm on the penultimate draft of a paper on another case of Alzheimer's with a new mutation. At thirty-five, she's one of the youngest patients I've ever seen. Where have you been? You don't normally come to the Royal Society of Medicine in the middle of the afternoon. Come to think of it, you don't often visit this institution at any time.'

'On the spur of the moment I decided to come to work in the library. To recover from a strange and unpleasant experience. I've just come – you wouldn't believe it – from Paddington Green Police Station. I wanted to see you anyway and would have called you from home later tonight. In fact, I was desperate to talk to you last night, but by the time I got home after the accident I was exhausted.'

'What accident? And what were you doing in the police station? What is this all about? Have you been spraying the lenses of the security cameras with water resistant paint? It was clearly not you who took a potshot at the President the day before yesterday. Shame that the poor woman missed.'

'You're right, it wasn't me. But it was one of my patients.'

'Joining the resistance by proxy?' Daniel looked at Mark and realised that his joke, despite the smile it elicited, was not best timed.

The tea break had ended and the conservatory had emptied, waiters were removing the remnants of the tea and only a couple of people lingered around the registration desk in the foyer. Mark and Daniel walked to the cafe opposite the restaurant, sat in a quiet corner and ordered coffee: cappuccino for Mark and espresso for Daniel.

For a while neither spoke. When he had spotted Daniel in the foyer, Mark could hardly wait to share his experience at the police station with him, but now he was reluctant to start. To gain time, he asked a question, leading back to the early stages of their friendship.

'Do you remember my first visit to your grandparents?'

'Yes, I do. But why do you ask this now?'

Mark did not answer; he did not know why. Only later did he understand the connection between two disparate events, separated by several years.

16

Mark remembered entering the ground floor flat in a Victorian house in West Hampstead, the heavy antique furniture, the good oil paintings and some fine aquarelles on the walls by painters he had never heard of, the ecru lace tablecloth, the fine Herend coffee cups in which strong coffee was served accompanied by poppy seed and ground walnut roulade: the specialty of the house, as Helen, Daniel's grandmother, had jokingly said, offering a plateful to the guest. It was a world alien to his, yet warm and accommodating.

Helen's husband, Tibor, was a small child when they escaped. One late November evening in 1956, his father had come home and told his wife to pack: they would be leaving tomorrow. They should not waste any time since the borders to Austria would be soon closed. Their flat was in central Budapest, on a side street which had been caught up in the crossfire between the Soviet tanks in the main avenue and the freedom fighters. As they were locking the door of their flat behind them, Tibor asked his father when they were coming back.

'Never,' was the curt answer.

Mark could hardly imagine this experience of people escaping from their home into the unknown because the fear, desperation and hopelessness in their life was greater than any uncertainty the future might bring. At the time he did not know that the Weisz family had had previous experience of losing their home when they had been herded to ghettos in the spring of 1944 soon after the German Army had invaded Hungary. Yet they were more fortunate than their provincial relatives, some of whom ended up in the concentration camp of Bergen-Belsen or in the gas chambers of Auschwitz.

For the first time in his life, from the stories of an old Hungarian Jew, the ghosts of recent European history had resurfaced to cast deep shadows over the hitherto unperturbed sunny upland of Mark's English youth. He had studied modern history at school, and James was also a more than average knowledgeable guide to continental upheavals, but listening to Daniel's grandfather was altogether a different experience: the urgency of the witness combined with the acuteness of the storytelling. Listening to Tibor Weisz he was mesmerised, but only later did he realise the importance of their encounter.

Their escape, although started rather conventionally, was nothing if not miraculous. To avoid suspicion, they had left all their possessions behind, packing only bare essentials and some food in a small weekend bag. Tibor's mother had sewn her jewellery into the lining of her winter coat: they were all wearing their warmest clothes.

Had they been stopped and questioned by the police, their story that they were visiting relatives in the county would have sounded plausible. As his father closed the door of their flat finally behind them, Tibor was seized by fear and remorse that he would never see his friends again. They walked to the Eastern Railway Station situated barely one mile from their flat, and took the first train to the west. At the last large stop before the border they managed to hire a taxi and asked the driver to take them to a village that was only a few miles from the border. Tibor's father had done his homework in advance and scouted out the easiest and safest place to cross into Austria.

From this village they had set out on foot towards the border. For Tibor the walk in the dark seemed never-ending. From time to time the night sky was illuminated by flares streaking across it in a blaze of light and extinguished on the horizon. He was terrified and clung to his father's hand. His mother was a few steps behind them. Yet he was fascinated by the daring of their escape and thrilled by the danger: it was an adventure, the like of which he had previously only read of in books. There were border guards and soldiers in the area, but more ominously they had picked up rumours in the village of the recent arrival of a Russian unit in the nearby town.

They navigated gingerly through a copse of trees in the dark. Heavy clouds obliterated the moon and the stars, but they did not dare switch on their torch for its light might attract the border guards' attention. Their feet sank deep into carpets of sodden leaves. They were paralysed by fear as rabbits suddenly jumped up to escape into the night.

The trees had thinned out behind them and they arrived in a clearing. The border must not be far now, they thought. Suddenly a shaft of light blinded them. They were frozen to the spot. Two border guards wearing Hungarian uniforms, appearing from nowhere, stood ten yards in front of them. They came closer: both were in their early twenties. One slowly focused the light on their faces one by one without saying a single word. Having finished the inspection, the guard holding the torch turned around, directing the light away from the three terrified figures into the thickness of night:

'That way is to the border. Good luck.' He switched off the torch and they were gone.

At dawn they were picked up by Austrian border guards, and deposited in one of the refugee camps outside Vienna that the Austrians had set up with international help to receive tens of thousands of Hungarians. From the temporary collection centres the refugees had later been dispersed to the four corners of the world. Their guardian angel in the camp was an eccentric charity worker in his late twenties who, despite his extraordinary name of Prince Arnold von Lobkowitz, was an English nurse from London. As the Weisz family later learned, he had been adopted by an Austrian aristocratic family when he was a child. He spoke a few words of Hungarian and had become fond of Tibor's father whose knowledge of Austro-Hungarian history impressed the Englishman.

It was von Lobkowitz who had helped to ease their passage

to England, asking where the family wished to go once the new quotas of immigration became available. Tibor's father chose England, a country he had admired and the only one in Europe that, according to him, had finished the war with honour. Living in England, they would remain in Europe but as far as possible from the communist satellites of the Soviet camp. Thus, the Weisz family of three had arrived on a windy January day.

The waitress brought their coffee. Mark turned to Daniel and finally recounted the events of the last couple of days.

'Honestly, I don't know whether Dufresne was behind the Research Council's decision to postpone my funding application, but the interview at Paddington Green was a Kafkaesque experience. Apparently, it was all about last night's accident.' For a second he hesitated whether to tell Daniel about the unexpected ending of his interview.

'You're such a good driver but there was a collision. It was hardly an accident though: incidences like this occur every day by the thousand. Your Morton seemed to be a decent bloke who didn't want to take it any further. If I had any doubt before that they had a hand in shelving your programme grant, it's now clear that they've decided to put pressure on you.'

'I'm afraid I have to agree,' sighed Mark with an air of resignation. 'If I had any uncertainty earlier, it was expelled today during my meeting with Blakemore. Unfortunately it became rather confrontational. He's convinced that I should collaborate with Dufresne, otherwise we won't have any funding for future research.'

'Does it mean,' Daniel started, but reading his thoughts, Mark pre-empted:

'Yes, it does. It means that I can finish the preliminary experiments, but once they are completed, however successful they are, I have to stop altogether. Curtains for my academic career. It may get even worse: with Dufresne one doesn't know. He really sends shivers down my spine.'

'You can't give up academic medicine altogether. That's too high a price to pay. I know that your initial reaction was to refuse him – and I understand your arguments more than anybody else – but perhaps you've got to reconsider your position. It isn't my field, but he has a cohort that otherwise you wouldn't be able to recruit. And knowing the nature of your research, this is halfway to success.' Mark remained silent: Daniel was right. For the first time he had to admit that the offer he had so abruptly dismissed earlier was an opportunity he ought to have seized. Daniel continued: 'By the way, what did Anne say? She has such a rational mind.'

'She is unequivocal that I should work with Dufresne. It's intriguing that Dufresne contacted her without any qualms.' Mark lifted his cup, then realising that he had already drunk his cappuccino, nervously replaced it on the saucer. Looking straight into Daniel's eyes, as if pinning him against a wall, he abruptly asked: 'In my position, would you collaborate with Dufresne?'

The question took Daniel by surprise. He raked his fingers through his hair, a gesture Mark had recognised a long time ago as a sign of nervousness. Daniel shifted his gaze from Mark. The cafe was quite busy, yet peaceful. Sinking into large armchairs or spreading over leather sofas, their colleagues conducted their conversations in hushed tones or buried their faces in the papers or more likely into their own manuscripts. Waitresses silently glided with their trays amongst the tables. The barman uncorked a bottle of white wine. Mark could not help feeling remorse for putting his friend on the spot. Finally, Daniel answered.

'I don't know. It's a damn difficult decision. But in the end, yes, I probably would. Not for saving my research, that wouldn't be good enough, but for being able to help those people.'

'Daniel, you amaze me. You come from a family who sacrificed everything for their freedom – they even risked their lives. And now you advise me to compromise my professional integrity! You of all people! I can't believe you.'

'Mark, have you considered, forgetting for a minute about Dufresne, where your breakthrough may lead?'

'What do you mean?'

'Well, you are going to publish your experiments as soon as your cohort is going to be statistically significant and your results are solid. Yes?'

'Of course. But what are you getting at?'

'Once this work becomes public knowledge, everyone with your expertise can use it. There might not be many people who are so qualified but there are some. A couple of months after publication Dufresne might find someone less scrupulous who will do the job for him.'

'I did think of this possibility.'

'There is also another aspect to thought modification. You can help patients enormously with personality disorders, but this methodology could be endlessly abused in the wrong hands.'

'Yes Daniel, I know. And yes, I have considered the implications. Is there anything new in this respect? Modern medicine has many variations on this theme. Drugs to heal can also poison people. Genetics can be misused and have been misused.'

'Mark, calm down. You've had a very stressful couple of days and now you should put Dufresne's offer into perspective. You aren't being asked to make a Faustian deal, you only have to choose the lesser of two evils. However, whatever you decide you must know that you can count on me.'

'To change the subject, something else emerged from the past rather out of the blue and completely unrelated to the accident during the interview. Perhaps I should have started with this terrible story, but I just wanted to calm down first. It isn't easy to talk about it, even to you. You will be shocked, I have to warn you.' Daniel listened to the story of his friend's first love: previously Mark had never mentioned Julia and a closed chapter of his friend's life opened up.

'Have you ever tried to see her again?'

'Yes, I did. The other medical student Julia shared a flat with in Bloomsbury told me that she'd moved out at short notice before the exams, without leaving a forwarding address. I tracked her parents down in Lancaster but they practically warned me off her: they were adamant that their daughter didn't want to see me or hear from me ever again. I couldn't do much else. Marriage wasn't an option. It was a traumatic experience: the feeling of guilt haunted me for a long time. Today Julia returned from the past to reclaim a place in my conscience from which I have tried to erase her. I can't help feeling that I am, at least partly, responsible for her death.'

'You are not! But it's natural that you feel guilty. Does Yasmina know about Julia?'

'No, she doesn't. Rightly or wrongly, I decided it wasn't relevant to our relationship.'

'Are you going to tell her now?'

'Perhaps Julia should remain our secret for the time being.' Without saying a word both felt that discussing this tragic episode of Mark's life had strengthened the bond between them.

Daniel suddenly changed the subject. 'What are you doing tonight? Why don't you and Yasmina come to have dinner with us? I could telephone Chris to find out whether we've food in the house, and even if the fridge is empty we could always go out.' Daniel suggested that they meet in their house off the Essex Road in Islington at eight o'clock.

Before leaving the cafe, Mark called Morton again. This time he was lucky, the pharmacologist answered: 'I received your message and was about to call you – I've just returned from work.' Mark could barely withhold his anger.

'I was interviewed at Paddington Green Police Station this afternoon on account of our encounter last night. You apparently made a complaint against me.'

There was silence at the other end. Morton must have been taken aback by Mark's directness and was considering his response. When it finally came, it did not surprise Mark:

'I was contacted by the police. They stated that the cameras picked up the accident and were surprised that we didn't report it. It was my duty, they said, to make a statement.'

'And did you?' There was yet more silence.

'They advised me to do so.'

Mark contemplated the nuances of meaning with which this verb could be invested.

'Did they also advise you to report the accident to your insurance company? We didn't find any damage worth reporting last night.'

'On a more thorough look in daylight, I did discover a dent on the back bumper which might have to be replaced.'

By now Mark was convinced that the police had pressurised Morton to report the accident to create an excuse, if they needed one, for his interview. Any further conversation was futile, and he brought the exchange to an abrupt end.

Stepping out into Wimpole Street, Mark hesitated to hail one of the passing black cabs, and chose to walk home. The rain had stopped, a warm wind dried the pavement and the setting sun made a fleeting appearance under threatening clouds in the western sky. From the corner of Cavendish Square he spared a glance at his favourite London sculpture: Epstein's *Madonna and Child* pinned to a stone arch between two Palladian buildings leading to what had once been a theological college. The unexpected meeting with Daniel and sharing the burden of his interview had helped to lift his gloom, and the serene beauty of the statue had filled him with confidence. Inexplicably, he had gained strength from pieces of stone – a woman protecting and yet at the same time offering her child to the world. For the first time that day he felt that he could face the trials which had come his way during the last forty-eight hours.

He turned into Harley Street. The private surgeries were closing: secretaries were clearing their desks and turning off the lights, couriers were collecting late reports, and the last patients were hailing taxis or getting into waiting limousines. Within half an hour the street would be deserted. He crossed Marylebone Road and the Outer Circle, and through one of the small cast iron gates he entered Regent's Park. The lights had suddenly faded and a fine drizzle started to fall. He quickened his steps; he did not want to get wet or to be stranded in the Park.

It was getting late: the gates of the Inner Circle were locked at dusk by the park's guards who drove around in a van closing the gates in an order unknown to evening visitors. That he might have to climb over the railing to get out, as occasionally had happened in the past, should have occurred to him earlier. But tonight he wanted to spare himself this acrobatic performance and quickened his pace. He was lucky, since one of the guards, seeing the lonely figure hurrying towards him, held the gate open to let him out.

Unexpectedly the drizzle turned into a heavy shower, and by the time he rushed down the few steps to the door of their house he had been drenched. The lights were on: Yasmina had arrived home earlier. The glare of the illuminated windows shining through the downpour offered a warm welcome.

17

Mark and Yasmina arrived at Chris and Daniel's house in Islington a few minutes after eight o'clock. Although it was not very far from smart Canonbury and the bustle of Islington Green, being on the eastern periphery of Islington, towards Hackney, the area had been gentrified later than the rest of the borough, and house prices had not started their astronomical climb until a couple years before the Olympic Games.

Their hosts' house was part of an early Victorian terrace: a handsome building on three floors with a basement. The light from the large ground floor window illuminated the small front garden in which a solitary magnolia tree stood in the centre of the lawn surrounded by a meticulously trimmed hedge of box. At the press of the bell Chris, a short stocky man in his early fifties, opened the door, standing in the shaft of light. He kissed Yasmina, shook Mark's hand, took their raincoats and hung them in the built-in wardrobe at the end of the narrow hall.

'Good to see you,' he said, as he ushered his visitors into the large living room. The entire ground floor had been transformed into a single space: the kitchen at the back continued into the spacious dining area with a large oblong table and six chairs. At the front, facing the street two sofas and two armchairs surrounding a large glass coffee table provided comfort for drinks before and for coffee after dinner. Built-in bookcases from floor to ceiling covered two walls. A glass panelled double door opened onto the brick-walled back garden.

'Daniel, the guests have arrived,' Chris shouted, but he had barely finished his sentence before Daniel entered the room.

'The two of you already had a cosy little tête-à-tête this

afternoon in the Royal Society of Medicine.' In the teasing, Mark could detect just a slight tension as Chris addressed him. He instinctively knew that Chris was jealous of his friendship with Daniel. He and Daniel were not only of the same age but also shared, both being clinical neuroscientists, a similar medical background and interests: it was the natural feeling of the older man who was excluded from their professional world.

'We're delighted that you could manage to join us tonight,' said Chris. He spoke with his habitual slight formality, but Mark knew the welcome was genuine. 'What would you like to drink? We could open a bottle of champagne. Mark, you've had a dreadful day – let's cheer you up.' While Daniel produced four flutes and poured the drink, Chris laid the table with plates of cold meats: slices of ham and rare roast beef accompanied by bowls of salad, a cheese board and a large loaf of bread. 'I didn't have time to cook – Daniel gave me such short notice,' he said apologetically, 'so you'll have to put up with a cold collation: the result of a last-minute shopping trip to the delicatessen.' Finally he produced two bottles of wine: the red had already been uncorked, while the bottle of Chablis, just removed from the fridge and brought into the warm room, was covered with condensation.

Mark had never forgotten the surprise he felt when he had met Chris for the first time. Soon after his encounter with Daniel at Wye College, he had suggested that Daniel should meet his fiancée. Mark and Anne had arrived a quarter of an hour before the agreed time. The bar was small and intimate; mercifully no background music spoiled the atmosphere.

'They're late,' said Anne disapprovingly, looking at her watch. She was one of the most disciplined people Mark knew, and being a stickler for punctuality she had always arrived on time and expected everybody else to do the same. Although he wanted to meet Daniel's partner, Mark suddenly regretted that he had agreed to the meeting. He could see Daniel in the foyer followed by a short stocky man. Mark and Anne stood up to welcome them.

'Anne, my fiancée,' said Mark.

'Chris, my partner,' said Daniel.

There was a momentary silence. Mark watched Anne. She was busily chatting away and from her initial response it was clear that they were going to get on well. As they all sat down and ordered more drinks there was no trace of tension or awkwardness. For Mark the real surprise was the age of Daniel's friend: Chris must have been Daniel's senior by more than ten years. As he learned later, the age difference was, in fact, fourteen years. At the time, he and Daniel were at the beginning of their professional careers. By contrast, Chris radiated the self-confident aura of a more mature man, someone who was already established. Mark's immediate response to Chris was not disapproval but mere curiosity. Why Daniel's choice had fallen on this podgy middle-aged man? As the evening unrolled Mark's question had been answered.

Drawn out by Anne's questioning, they learned that Chris was an Anglican priest. He had been trained in St Stephen's House, or the 'House' as this Anglican theological foundation in the University of Oxford was affectionately known. His first appointment was in a church in one of the run-down areas of east London where he was ordained to a curacy for three years. Just as his appointment was about to come up for renewal, the opportunity of a posting in Uganda for one year had given him a vantage point to observe the schism between the liberal and the evangelical wings of the Church, which spurred him on to pursue an academic career in theology on his return to England. He registered for a part-time PhD course at King's College London, and at the same time set out to find a parish that would allow him to work on his degree.

Soon after he had obtained his PhD, he was appointed lecturer in the Theology Department of King's College, a coveted position in a prestigious place. He became an undisputed expert on the relationship between the State and the Church and many years later, when the question of the disestablishment of the Anglican Church was seriously debated, he was invited to serve on the committee convened to prepare a report for the Synod.

At dinner on the day they had all met for the first time – they had moved from the bar into one of the Italian restaurants on Charlotte Street where they could get a table without a reservation – Anne asked Chris how they had met. Mark was taken aback by Anne's directness.

'Anne is an advocate, she must know everything,' he said apologetically but Daniel and Chris were happy to satisfy Anne's curiosity. They had met five years before on a Sunday evening at a charity concert held in support of AIDS research in a church opposite Waterloo station. Chris had just returned from Africa where the disease, despite the fact that the rate of infection had levelled off and begun to decline, was still a major health issue.

Daniel was at the time reviewing archival cases of AIDS: he was particularly interested in the effects of antiviral medication on the brain. Research had revealed substantial nerve cell loss in the brains of patients who had died of AIDS; this damage, caused by the virus, was now nowhere to be seen, as a result of antiviral therapy.

From the sofa they moved to the table where Chris sliced the bread and Daniel poured the wine, while Yasmina passed the plate of cold meats and salad bowls around. The conversation turned from the renewal of Pinter's *Birthday Party*, which they all had seen recently in the West End, to Mark's visit to the police station.

'If you think that your interview at Paddington Green was anything extraordinary, think again,' said Chris after Mark had finished his story. 'We have reports, although not all corroborated, that the police use these interviews to intimidate people – anybody who becomes slightly suspicious. Law and order must be maintained at all costs.'

'Don't you think that you might be exaggerating slightly?' asked Yasmina.

'Yasmina, don't be so naïve. On Sunday the engineers from Home Security arrived in our street and put up a couple of voice sensitive cameras at the crossing towards the end of the road. With this new addition, we counted eighteen cameras in this short leafy street, and there may be many more, some hidden. And this is just the mere tip of a very large iceberg.' Chris drew a deep breath: he was on a subject close to his heart.

'The information from the cameras is linked up with other methods of potential surveillance: the internet, mobile and landline telephony, the global positioning system, facial recognition, and spy satellites that can scan every square yard of the ground. The State doesn't make any secret of the fact that, one way or another, we're being watched twenty-four hours of the day, every day of the year.

'One can argue that this is nothing new. Close circuit television cameras were apparently used temporarily in 1953 at the coronation of Queen Elizabeth II. Then the debit and credit cards arrived. Followed by the store loyalty cards. The recognition of car registration plates. The travel and library cards. The National Insurance Register. The NHS patients' records. The electoral rolls. Radio frequency identification tags in shops. Passports that for some time included biometric data. Not to mention the National DNA Database, the most comprehensive in existence. For a long time Britain has been, with China, the most observed country in the world.'

Daniel interjected: 'Chris, you're getting carried away on your favourite hobbyhorse. You forget that you're not giving one of your lectures on the malign growth of the Surveillance State.' But Chris ignored Daniel's remark.

'In a document I drew up last week, we stated that for the first time all these fragments of information have been integrated into a comprehensive, all seeing, all knowing nationwide surveillance system. The individual pieces have now fallen into place: the jigsaw has been completed. The State, if it so wishes, can observe, record and recall a twenty-four hour narrative of our life. The demarcation between private life and public authority, a delicate but well-guarded frontier formed as much by tradition and precedence as by legislation during centuries, has been progressively eroded.

'If they are interested in you,' and now Chris turned to Mark, 'and your visit to Paddington Green leaves very little doubt they are – they know that you're, at this moment, visiting us. They even know the food we are eating and the wine we are drinking from my credit card profile.

'Next time I go to visit the wine store in Upper Street, one of the assistants might ask whether I would like to have some of the Chablis Premier Cru 2032 and the Fleurie 2038, the wines we're drinking now. My identity on my PID, which he could read as I went in on the screen in front of him, is connected with the last purchase on my credit card. One could argue that this is simply efficient housekeeping, and I shouldn't mind if Johnny Bloggs in the wine store keeps a tab on our drinking habits. But at the same time, you must be aware that every aspect of our life has become an open book to the State. And this I do mind.' Chris stopped for a second and Mark used this brief pause to intervene:

'Chris, you said that you were getting reports. Whom are you referring to? And how do you get these reports?'

'The Church gets reports of intimidation and harassment. The Church of England hasn't yet been abolished and congregations, although they might be bugged, aren't yet monitored. And there are priests who are opposed to what is happening.'

'Before my interview in Paddington Green I had a few minutes to while away, and on the spur of moment I did something I haven't done for a long time: I visited a church and found the experience strangely soothing. It also made me think.' The others looked at him, waiting for some explanation but none was forthcoming. Mark paused, and sipped his wine. His next question took Chris by surprise: 'Do you think it was a mistake to disestablish the Church of England?'

Chris answered with another question: 'Do you think that if the Church had remained part of the Establishment it could have had a stronger influence on the Government? Frankly, I don't think so. It had become necessary to separate the Church from the State. At the time it was thought by many influential voices in the hierarchy that by severing the umbilical cord the Anglican Congregation would be able to pursue a more independent course.

'In a way this is exactly what has happened. The Church has been in freefall for some time with dwindling congregations and accelerating desecration of places of worship. At the last count in 2038, attendances had fallen to their lowest level at just under 400,000 and with the closure of more than 6,000 churches during the last twenty-five years only some 10,000 have remained open. Yet during the last couple of years the trend has been reversed. Sunday attendances have been increasing as if people are returning to the Church for guidance and protection.'

Having finished their meal, they moved back to the living area. Daniel brewed some coffee, and Chris produced a plate of fresh fruit and a box of chocolates. As they settled on the sofas and armchairs, Chris turned to Mark:

'Shall we return to your case for a moment? From now on they will pay particular attention to you. The interview in Paddington Green, you must know, was a way of putting the screws on you. You should try to talk to the driver of the other car, although I doubt that he will volunteer the information that he changed his mind because the boys from Home Security put pressure on him. Possibly they might have had information by which they could have blackmailed Morton. Dufresne will do his best to get your collaboration. Your expertise would be invaluable to him. Home Security will claim that by medical help they would eliminate dangerous crime and terrorism.' Having drunk his coffee, Chris warmed to his subject and continued:

'No more threats of explosions and no more suicide bombers. No more riots, violent muggings and gratuitous violence. Murder rates and all indicators of serious crime would go down. The Surveillance State has paid handsome dividends – we are soon going to live in a society without crime. We've made a compromise: for safety and security, for law and order we surrendered our freedom and human rights. The question is – was it worth it?'

His last sentence hung in the air: no answer was warranted.

'Is there any alternative?' asked Yasmina.

'You remember you are free, in a way, to opt out of the system. You can surrender your Personal Identity Database. In doing so you lose your identity in the machinery of the State. For bureaucracy you become a non-person. You may not be able to travel abroad. You will become unemployable and you lose your pension rights. You won't have medical assistance and can't take out an insurance policy. You don't have access to a bank and you lose your credit and debit cards. All access to electronic communication will be barred: no internet connection, no e-mail and no search engines. You won't be able to get hold of an increasing number of books published only electronically.'

'Has anybody ever elected to opt out of the system?' asked Yasmina. 'One can't exist without a PID.'

'You'd be surprised. There are some people who have refused to carry the Database. The Government maintains a silence about these dissenters, since their existence hasn't been formally acknowledged. Officially they are referred to as PWIs or Persons Without Identity.'

Mark abruptly looked up from his empty coffee cup which he was about to refill. Yes, he thought with instant recognition, these are the people Fiona Cartwright was enthusing about and in whose lifestyle he had not shown much interest at the time. He remembered how disappointed his patient had been at his lukewarm response. Presently, he put down the empty cup and, with his interest aroused, concentrated on Chris.

'Their way of life is a peaceful resistance to the Government. There are a few groups scattered in the country, usually in small provincial towns or villages, living in loosely organised communes. One of the nearest to London is in Whitstable in Kent.'

'That's it,' exclaimed Mark. They all turned towards him, surprised by his sudden exclamation.

'I'm sorry,' he apologised, 'but this is such an odd coincidence. Fiona Cartwright, the woman in the stadium, mentioned these people and their commune in Whitstable.' Chris nodded as if indicating his forgiveness for the unwarranted interruption.

'I know one of the local priests, Alex Beresford, who, although he isn't a member, is an active supporter of the community. If you want, we could organise a little excursion to visit them next weekend.'

Mark was enthusiastic about the idea and they agreed to travel to Whitstable the following Saturday. By the time they had finished their coffee it was after midnight and they decided to call a taxi. They did not have to wait long: the car arrived within the promised ten minutes. Entering the taxi, there was no need to give their address to the driver. Their identity had been scanned and they could see as it appeared on the screen below their name on the GPS: 11 Cambridge Place, NW1 4NB.

'I look forward to meeting these people in Whitstable,' said Mark as they sat back in the cab.

18

The telephone jolted him out of his sleep. The familiar sound had taken on a brutal urgency early in the morning. The night before they had arrived home late from Daniel and Chris's and it was well after one o'clock by the time they switched off the light. It took Mark a few seconds to resurface from his deep sleep. When he came to his senses, he still felt it was the middle of the night. The room was enveloped in darkness: the light of dawn had not yet penetrated through the ill-fitting shutters. The old-fashioned mechanical bedside clock showed ten past six.

It was James. His voice was faltering but at the same time it came through with a matter-of-fact simplicity: 'Mark ... Clarissa died during the night.'

'I'll be with you as soon as I can.' He could not say anything else for consoling words were meaningless and he knew that James did not need them.

The news of Clarissa's death was not entirely unexpected: Mark had followed her physical and mental deterioration with a mixture of sadness and helplessness. He knew more than anybody else that there was nothing he could do. There were the moments when he felt that he was wasting his time: he had made the wrong decision and regretted that he had ever become a doctor. What is the use of the work I do, he questioned, when I can't help someone I love? These periods of doubt were, however, short-lived, yet he was still apprehensive that one day this fear of helplessness might overwhelm him.

With the light now on, he woke Yasmina. Within a few minutes they were both ready to leave the house: foregoing breakfast, they had time only for a quick shower and a cup of coffee.

The streets were deserted. The morning rush hour had not yet started and the drive to Belgravia took less than a quarter of an hour. James was waiting for them and as they hurried up the stairs he was already standing in the open door of the flat. He hugged both Mark and Yasmina. Behind him at the end of the hall stood Agnieta. As Mark kissed her, he saw her in a different light. For the first time she was an elderly woman with greying hair and bloodshot eyes; she had obviously been crying.

Mark followed James into the bedroom, while Yasmina and Agnieta stopped at the door. He walked to the bed and in a gesture, as automatic to a doctor seeing a body immediately after death as it was futile, he felt Clarissa's pulse, before kissing her forehead. As he looked at her he could not fail to notice that in death Clarissa had regained some of the beauty ravaged by age and disease. Her face was peaceful. Her features, which had been contorted by anguish and fear in life, were smoothened out, and her lips which in recent months had uttered only incomprehensible fragments of speech, were sealed for ever. As he bent over his grandmother's face he could see a couple of drops of sweat on her temple. Her eyes had been closed earlier.

'She died suddenly,' said James, 'between four and six o'clock. At four when I went to the bathroom, she was still alive – I could hear her snoring. A few minutes before six I went down to the kitchen to make tea. When I got back to the bedroom, I didn't switch on the lights, I put the tray with the teapot and the two mugs on my bedside table. We always have weak China or fruit tea in the morning. Neither of us takes any milk or sugar.' James suddenly stopped, not knowing why he had uttered this irrelevant information.

They moved to the drawing room. Always ready to help, Agnieta offered to make breakfast but they all declined it; only Yasmina asked for a glass of orange juice.

'She died so suddenly,' repeated James. 'Her death was so unexpected.'

Mark looked at James and then Yasmina as if asking for help. He wanted to say that Clarissa's sudden death, however painful for them with its swift arrival, had spared her from further suffering. Her decline, intellectual and physical, was irreversible; in a way she had already departed. He saw that Yasmina was crying, silently. He wanted to console her but did not know what to say. Instead, he embraced her. To overcome his grief, Mark concentrated on dealing with the practicalities of death.

'We should ring the GP. She will issue a death certificate.'

'I've already done that, but of course the surgery doesn't open today until ten. I left a message on Dr Mahinder's private line, asking her to call me back as soon as possible.'

An unspoken agreement was tacitly acted upon: as long as they both adhered to discussing the arrangements, they could postpone talking about their feelings. It was the natural escape of those who have been accustomed to a well-ordered professional life: solace and satisfaction in efficiently carried out tasks. They were also reassured by the knowledge that each knew the other's feelings, and could draw strength from the other's company.

Mark was aware that James immensely disliked public displays of private grief. He made scathing comments about the emotional incontinence of the English. How could mothers, facing the limelight of cameras, cry into the lens about their recently deceased children? It was indecent to share their loss with millions of viewers. The telephone rang. James answered: it was Anthony.

'He's arriving at St Pancras at 12.30 next Monday. He's sorry for not being able to come sooner but he'll be with us a couple of days before the funeral. Hélène will join him later, immediately after she has managed to fix up someone to supervise the nanny.'

The thought of his brother's arrival lightened Mark's mood: they had not seen each other for several weeks, and Mark felt a sudden urge not only to share his grief with him but also to confide in Anthony.

The telephone rang again and this time Mark answered it.

'Yes, Dr Mahinder, that's fine. Yes, I'll tell him.' He hung up and turned to James.

'Mahinder will be here within half an hour.'

When the bell rang Mark let the GP in. She expressed her condolences and without wasting further time, she proceeded to Clarissa's bedroom. She examined her patient: a superficial survey of a lifeless body to acknowledge the presence of death. A short but necessary protocol which took only a couple of minutes, performed with tact and dignity. She completed the death certificate, telephoned the undertakers and was gone. Bronchopneumonia, she stated, was the condition directly leading to death, resulting from dementia associated with Parkinson's disease. With the death certificate signed, James and Mark could begin to plan Clarissa's funeral.

19

After some discussion Yasmina and Mark had decided to carry on with their planned trip to Whitstable. Anne had promised to call on James on both days of the weekend and Agnieta was going to stay in the flat to keep him company. Mark thought that his grandfather might need a little time to get used to his new status without having to comfort him and Yasmina.

They met Daniel and Chris at Victoria Station at nine thirty on Saturday morning. The fast service took twenty minutes to reach Whitstable. The train stopped only once in Rochester, allowing a quick glance at the panorama of the castle majestically brooding over the Medway. Before they reached their final destination the undulating countryside flattened out and the sea swam into view: grey, cold and uninviting under the cloudy sky.

'Tell us a little bit about Alex Beresford,' Mark turned to Chris as the train approached the station.

'Alex is an old friend from St Stephen's House days. Although we pursued entirely different careers within the Church of England, we kept in touch throughout the years. He's quite a character. Even before he was ordained, Alex married and I was his best man. His ambition, he explained on the day of his wedding, didn't exceed a quiet parish in rural England and a happy family life. In this he has been quite successful: in the parish of All Saints in Whitstable and in the person of Sally Watts, a French teacher in Canterbury, he fulfilled his aspirations. She delivered three children in rapid succession, and I'm the godfather of the firstborn. The rest you're going to see for yourselves.'

From the station they walked down to the harbour. By the time they reached the waterfront the sun had dispersed the cover of low-lying grey clouds and the weather, as if making amends for the previous week's rain, turned warm and sunny. The town had never built a grand promenade and perhaps as a consequence had not developed into a proper seaside resort, thus preserving most of its natural beauty. Creosoted weatherboard houses on the seafront were bathed in sunshine. In front of several beach huts the owners enjoyed their morning coffee, while the more enterprising were preparing a picnic lunch. Young professional couples, escaping the capital and known by the locals as DFLs or Down from London, were pushing old-fashioned prams or exercising their dogs. A group of teenage boys was throwing pebbles on the surface of the water: most of the missiles sank but an occasional one ricocheted a couple of times over the surface before finally submerging. White horses, whipped up earlier by strong east winds, had died down and the sparkling greenish-blue sea was inviting but far too cold for swimming.

They stopped on the pebbly beach, mesmerised by the brilliance in front of them, breathing in the salty sea air redolent of smoked fish. Screeching seagulls nosedived for their prey and as they hit their target fish glinted in their remorseless beaks on the takeoff from the sea. Despite the surroundings, Mark felt numb. He could barely believe that Clarissa was dead. His present concerns seemed almost trivial. Whatever he decided he would never be able to help her now, however advanced research had become.

They decided to take a walk along the coast to work up an appetite. Mark felt as if he were in a bubble and preferred to walk separately from Yasmina, even when she tried to take his hand. The choice of where to eat was not difficult: a flight of steps from the fish market led up to a restaurant renowned not only for its outstanding food but also for its commanding view of the harbour.

Following lunch they went to locate their bed and break-fast places, which Chris had booked the night before at Alex

Beresford's recommendation. It was not difficult to find them, since they were staying in adjacent houses, just off Harbour Street. Alex Beresford had invited Chris and Daniel to stay in the vicarage, but they had politely turned him down. He even apologised that he could not extend the invitation to Mark and Yasmina, but there was only one guest bedroom in the vicarage.

In the end they had accepted an invitation for Saturday dinner. Chris assured his friends that Sally Beresford was an outstanding cook: while staying in France she had not only become fluent in French but had also gained considerable skill in the kitchen.

The vicarage was large but without the mustiness, cold-ness and barely disguised sadness which sometimes becomes ingrained in these places. The house was full of warmth and vitality as if it had absorbed the personality of those people who had been living there.

'It will be an unapologetically fishy dinner,' Sally warned, 'but we are after all in a seaport.' And she produced a meal of seared scallops with mushy peas and garlic mash followed by baked halibut with a lentil salad and finished off with cold lemon soufflé and toasted almonds. The conversation soon turned to the local community of PWIs.

'Who are these people? Where are they from? What do they want? And why are they in Whitstable?' Mark asked, glancing at Yasmina and feeling suddenly how pleased he was that she was there with him. They were kindred spirits.

'Thank you for reminding me, I nearly forgot to tell you. We've invited a young couple for coffee and after-dinner drinks. They will answer your questions far better than I can. But in the mean-time you have to put up with me. Why in Whitstable, indeed. A few years ago, soon after PIDs were introduced to replace bio-metric identity cards, there was a much-publicised case of an elderly couple living in Whitstable who refused to carry the per-sonal database. I don't even think that their resistance was a con-scious political gesture: they were simply eccentrics who weren't enamoured with the idea of being tagged. And by coincidence, they happened to live in my parish.

'The reprisal, a much publicised trial, was intended to be a stark warning of the dire consequences if any citizen should reject the implant of the Personal Identity Database. The Government,' Beresford went on, 'wanted to create an example to deter all potential dissenters. The hardships heaped upon them were immense: they would have to live outside society. They would become non-entities, people who don't exist. Citizens would be denied all the benefits of an affluent, secure existence. It was at this time that the term Person Without Identity or PWI was coined.'

Listening to Beresford, all of a sudden Mark made connections. Daniel's grandparents were prepared to surrender their past and to leave everything behind: their larger family and friends, their home and livelihood. They were risking the unknown, possible arrest and even death, all for the promise of freedom. The sacrifice of PWIs was so much less demanding, yet they also accepted hardship to escape the all-embracing interference of the State.

Beresford took a sip from his wine and then continued: 'But the publicity campaign backfired. The trial had created interest in the old couple and soon visitors arrived who were less interested in Whitstable's excellent oysters and seafood but more in this couple. You know how these things happen. The media, still relatively independent at the time, took up their case and overnight they had become symbols of resistance. By the way, the old couple, Gregory and Jessica Bentley, are still living outside town in the same cottage their family has owned for centuries. When the Government put pressure on them, they took their case to the European Court of Justice and after two years of legal tussle they won. Their victory wasn't much advertised by the media, which was by then controlled by Home Security.'

The guests listened intently to Beresford. Mark could vaguely recall the case as he caught Yasmina's eye. In agreement they both simultaneously nodded. Before Fiona Cartwright first mentioned their existence they were ignorant of the fact that small communities had sprung up composed of people whose only cause was resistance to being tagged with Personal Identity Databases. This was the first time they had heard someone who not only knew these people personally, but had also been actively involved in their affairs.

Following the Bentleys' legal victory more people arrived, Beresford told them, and they bought a few properties outside town including a couple of orchards a few miles away. A solicitor who specialised in human rights also settled with his wife and two children, and soon he became a figurehead: a natural leader, a man with considerable charisma who gradually organised a small commune of self support. A general practitioner who lived in Canterbury joined them and later they also recruited a dentist.

'What are they living on? What is their source of income?' Mark asked.

Beresford explained that the group became self-sufficient in food, producing more fruit and vegetables than they needed for their own consumption and selling the surplus at the local market at premium prices. On one of the farms they have been raising livestock, including chickens, ducks and geese, and some of these also found their way to the market or got snapped up by local restaurants for their superior quality. 'They don't seem to be short of money,' Beresford smiled. He paused and the others looked at him, as if nudging him to get on with his story.

'You may have heard of Colin Bates?' Chris and Daniel nodded.

'Isn't he a painter?' Daniel asked. 'I seem to remember that he had an exhibition of seascapes, some oils but chiefly watercolours, quite recently. Wasn't it in one of the Cork Street galleries? We didn't go but the reviews were excellent.'

'Yes, he's the man. What the critics probably forgot to mention was that he joined the commune here two years ago. He's also one of the conscientious objectors.'

'Conscientious objectors? Isn't that rather an old-fashioned term?' interrupted Mark.

'Yes, it is. With echoes from the First World War, but it's the term they prefer. It is their rejection of the official label of Person Without Identity. Bates's pictures, as you might guess, go for quite large sums of money and his last exhibition was a sell-out. Being a philanthropist, he has donated practically all the proceeds to the commune.

'One of the pictures over the writing desk between the windows is his.' While Sally remained seated, the guests stood up to look at the picture. It was an abstract aquarelle, all shining in shades of blue: the azure of the sea imperceptibly merging with the cerulean sky of the vanishing perspective. Yet it was the same sea they had all gazed at several hours ago, easily recognisable, lifted from its perpetual movements to be frozen in eternity.

'What a beautiful picture!' Mark exclaimed spontaneously. 'It breathes freedom and one is drawn into the limitless blueness of the open horizon.'

'No, I didn't buy the picture – I couldn't have afforded it,' added Beresford answering an unspoken question. 'A Christmas present from the artist. For services rendered. A very generous and much appreciated gesture.'

As they went back to the armchairs around the fireplace, Sally produced some freshly brewed coffee. The doorbell rang, and Alex Beresford jumped to his feet to usher in his guests, a couple in their late thirties.

'Brian and Harriet Downey. Your timing is perfect – coffee is just being served. Would you like a postprandial – brandy, liqueur or port?'

'No, thank you. Coffee would be fine,' the newcomers answered in unison.

After introductions they resettled around the fireplace. With one chair short, Yasmina perched on the side of the sofa next to Mark, wrapping her arm around his shoulder.

In this jovial atmosphere, the Downeys were relaxed enough to talk about their new life. Before moving to Whitstable, Brian had been a political correspondent with one of the online dailies, while Harriet had worked for a charity that monitored the welfare of prisoners. The year after the State of Emergency was declared, the charity had closed down, proclaiming lack of financial support, but it was an open secret that pressure from the Home Office played a greater part than shortage of funds. Brian had also objected to the editorial interference with his work. Their decision to leave London was a mixture of disillusion and expediency.

Mark was fascinated by their story. He tried to imagine himself in their shoes; after all, Brian and Harriet were only a few years their senior. Yet it was a life difficult to envisage.

'What happens if any member of the commune needs medical assistance beyond the ability of a general practitioner?' asked Mark. He was thinking of Clarissa, but he decided not to burden the rest of the company with the sad news. Instead he enlarged on the theme by saying, 'A heart attack for example, or appendicitis or a kidney transplant? Not plugged into the National Database, you aren't part of the health care system and in principle you aren't entitled to medical help.'

Brian was ready with the answer: 'There have been a couple of precedents in the past. In the last resort it is at the discretion of the consultant in charge, who decides whether the patient is admitted to a hospital or not. In years gone by, they have always been admitted and the patients paid. As you know a medical practitioner isn't going to refuse help to a patient in acute need. After all, the Hippocratic Oath must take precedence over the diktat of the State.'

'How do you manage your finances if you don't have a bank account?' asked Yasmina.

'This was more of a problem at the beginning. Instead of credit cards we simply use cash. We take plastic for granted but credit cards are relatively recent inventions: a hundred years ago or so they didn't exist. Or debit cards for that matter. It was more difficult to circumvent the problem of making investments. The way of bypassing the system is to set up family trusts to arrange investment by relatives. Apparently this route had been successfully explored.'

Beresford interrupted: 'One can't escape the irony of what has been happening. You might have noticed by now that the Government has quite unwittingly initiated a very exciting social experiment.'

Chris, looking at the carriage clock on the mantelpiece, realised with alarm that it was nearly midnight. 'We must go – it's getting very late.' He stood up and the others followed. They thanked the Beresfords for an enjoyable and stimulating evening and the Downeys for allowing them a glimpse of their life.

Back in their bed and breakfast room Mark felt a sudden and deep longing for Clarissa and wanted to talk about her. Yet, he said nothing. Instead, he turned to Yasmina who was undressing in preparation for her shower and asked suddenly: 'Would you like to live in the country?' A deep weariness with London and the life he would have to live in the future enveloped him. Taking her sweater off Yasmina's head presently disappeared in the tunnel of knitwear but even when she re-emerged with the urgency of a diver resurfacing for oxygen, she remained silent. Still startled, she replied, 'Are you serious?'

'I don't know. Moving to the country would be a profound change. As you know, I'm a Londoner through and through: born, studied and practised there, and until today I've never even considered living anywhere else.'

Yasmina nodded. She knew that Mark's love of the countryside did not extend beyond weekend excursions to East Anglia or to the Cotswolds or longer breaks of driving to the Scottish Highlands or to Cornwall.

'In the country my life would stand on its head. I wouldn't be able to continue my work and I'd have to retrain in order to get a general practice in a rural area. But we could leave the stress behind and not only would we get rid of Dufresne but also the pressures of academic medicine.' He wanted to explain how hopeless he felt in the face of Clarissa's death, but something held him back. He didn't want Yasmina to think his motives were weak. 'If I can't continue my research – and according to Blakemore this is now a real possibility – I would seriously consider moving to the country. And there is another factor to take into account. In the country it would be so much easier to bring up children. Better schools and a less stressful environment.'

'Do you mean opting out altogether like members of Beresford's commune?'

'Yes. And if I did, would you join me?'

'I would think about it,' answered Yasmina, smiling, 'but shall we forget about children for the time being?' By now naked, she walked to Mark, who was still standing by the window, embraced him and began slowly to undress him.

20

The Eurostar train from Paris due to arrive at 12.30 at St Pancras was on time. Mark had checked the electronic arrivals board on the lower concourse, and with ten minutes to spare, he ordered an espresso in one of the cafes. He could not fail to observe the large number of policemen milling around in the crowd; in addition to the Metropolitan Police, members of the Border Police, a special unit of Home Security could easily be picked out by their striking uniforms.

He took the escalator to the upper hall: a neo-Gothic cathedral erected as a tribute to the age of steam and restored during the first decade of the twenty-first century. As the train pulled in, he took up position at the barrier of international arrivals. Abruptly the deserted platform came alive as passengers hurried to get cleared by immigration control.

From a distance Mark could see two queues forming at the barrier: one for British citizens and one for all others. Since Britain had left the disintegrating European Union, passport holders of the previous member states had lost their right to pass through immigration with British citizens. Mark knew from previous experience that it might take some time for Anthony to get through, since his brother, even after living in France for nearly six years, had travelled on a British passport, maintaining his citizenship. However, he refused to have a PID.

All of a sudden, Mark became aware of shouting and scuffles on the other side of the barrier. A couple of minutes later, a middle-aged, well-dressed couple were being led by the Border Police. As they were escorted away, Mark could hear their protest in a thick French accent about the validity of their visa to enter the United Kingdom.

While waiting for Anthony, Mark sought refuge in recalling episodes of their childhood, escaping momentarily from the thoughts of Clarissa's death and Dufresne's menace. He could not help smiling at the thought of their rivalry for James and Clarissa's love, but above all for Agnieta's whose favours they desperately sought, keeping her prize cakes in mind. In this competition Mark felt the loser, for his shyness and awkwardness was not a match for his brother's charm and affability. At the age of ten Anthony had followed him to the City of London School for Boys, and it was only here that Mark could hold his own ground. His exam results were regularly better than his younger brother's.

Yet, Mark remained jealous since Anthony seemed to have sailed through the turbulence of adolescence with greater ease, arriving into the arms of his first stable girlfriend at the age of sixteen. For Mark it was a painful process and although by then he had overcome his physical clumsiness with regular exercise, he lost his virginity only during the summer vacation before his eighteenth birthday. When they had shared the house in Cambridge Place, Mark had observed Anthony's more easygoing, more relaxed attitude to life, to his studies and girlfriends and later to his work, with cool detachment but not without a touch of envy. It was not as if Anthony shunned his commitments and responsibilities, since he was loyal to his friends and won a prize at the Architectural Association while he was a student. But he had simply been blessed with the ability to inject an element of fun into everything he did.

After a few minutes Mark could see Anthony emerging from behind the barrier. The two brothers embraced. Apart from being of about the same height, they could not have been more different. Anthony had short-cropped blond hair, designer stubble, brown eyes and a hooked nose dominating his small lips. The loosely tailored light grey suit, with a polka-dotted dark grey handkerchief tumbling out of the breast pocket of the double vented jacket over a cornflower blue silk shirt, emphasised the artistic aura which he carefully cultivated and projected with ease and self-confidence, and not without a hint of theatricality. He was more animated than his brother, and even as he walked through the barrier, his arms, wide open and ready to embrace Mark, were a gesture to attract attention. Anthony was hardly dressed for a funeral, Mark thought, but then he noticed the smart suit carrier that would contain, no doubt, the obligatory black.

'The bloody buggers,' were Anthony's first words and when Mark looked at him questioningly, he continued, 'the Border Police. I refuse to be stapled like an experimental animal with a Personal Identity Database. I still have my old-fashioned pass-port. Fingerprints and irises and all that. But this clearly didn't satisfy the swine! They wanted to know everything. Or rather they wanted to confirm everything they already knew. They asked where I was staying. When I gave the Belgravia address, they asked whether I was coming for my grandmother's funeral. It didn't take them long to find out.'

'As soon as Dr Mahinder signed the death certificate the information would have been in the central computer system.'

'It may sound ridiculous but arriving in London is never without a fair dose of trauma. One is treated like a suspicious alien bent on causing harm to the earthly paradise of the new Republic.'

Mark found Anthony's outburst amusing. Whether the voice sensitive cameras would also find it amusing was a different matter. As they walked to the line of waiting taxis outside the station Anthony finally said, remembering the purpose of his trip: 'I'm so sorry. Tell me what happened.'

As the taxi made its way towards Belgravia, Mark gave an account of Clarissa's last days, expanding on James's brief report with some medical details. When he had finished, there was a pause.

'I can barely bring myself to say it,' responded Anthony, 'but her sudden death was a release from the clutches of that dreadful dementia. It must also be a relief to James and to you. I'd love to forget the memory of my last visit four or five weeks ago. It was a terrible shock to see the beautiful and sparkling Clarissa of our childhood becoming an incoherent and incontinent wreck. I'm ashamed, but I don't regret that I didn't see her more frequently.'

'I understand and certainly can't blame you.' Yet Mark had often missed his brother. He had needed him to share his anxiety and the pain he felt over Clarissa's disintegration. It had been a gradual process he could not reverse but their relationship had irreversibly changed over the years. Anthony's departure to France, a temporary venture at the time but by now a permanent fact of life, had loosened the ties between them.

The centrifugal forces of distance and time, the acquiring of new friends unknown to the other and the different problems of everyday life they had to face had pulled them apart, creating a gap which had been bridged from time to time only by the land-marks of life: birthdays and christenings, celebrations of pro-fessional achievements and now death. Their brief visits across the Channel were hardly satisfactory even to catch up with each other's news.

At Anthony's suggestion they had organised a joint holiday in the south of France a couple of years before, but that week in the hills behind Nice in a rented house with a large garden and swimming pool was less than an unqualified success. At the time Hélène, Anthony's wife, was in the advanced stages of preg-nancy: the birth of their second child was imminent. Muriel, their daughter, being just two years old, had craved a great deal of attention and when it was not granted fully to her satisfac-tion, she threw endless tantrums. The anxious parents had been preoccupied with the movements of their children: the one pre-cariously wandering around in the sloping garden, sometimes on all fours, the other whose kicking in the womb was carefully monitored.

In the oppressive heatwave at the end of August, the brothers did not have much time for each other. Earlier during that year

Mark's marriage had unravelled, and only when he and Anthony stole a couple of hours to drive down to the coast for a real swim in the sea could he talk about his problem with Anne and the appearance of Yasmina in his life.

'When is Hélène coming?' asked Mark. He was looking forward to the visit of his sister-in-law with an equal measure of expectation and trepidation. Personally, he could get on well with Hélène, but he was always aware of an air of unease between her and Yasmina. When asked, Yasmina first gave a non-committal answer and would only admit at repeated questionings that she had sometimes found Hélène overbearing. Hélène was a committed socialist, a fact that had never prevented her from enjoying the luxuries of a bourgeois life, underwritten by the lucrative architectural practice of her husband. Her more extreme views, apparently even left of the official line of the French Communist Party, irritated Yasmina. It was usually Anthony's quick intervention that prevented potential political arguments.

'Unfortunately she can't come until tomorrow. She's made arrangements for the children, asking her sister to supervise the nanny for a day or two.' Muriel was now four and Guy two, and Mark, who had become the godfather of the firstborn, joked with the parents that they had chosen names which could be used in both countries, although pronounced differently, for the sake of *entente cordiale*. He longed to see them, but the funeral was clearly not the occasion.

'How is work?' asked Mark, painfully aware of how little time he and Anthony had together.

'It's very busy. I can now afford to be choosy and to select clients with the more challenging projects.'

Anthony never made a secret of his conviction that his move to France was the best decision he had ever made. Increasingly disillusioned with his work in London, he rebelled against being an anonymous cog in the large machinery of an international firm, employing hundreds of architects. At the earliest opportunity that presented itself in the form of a job, offered by a small but reputable French architectural studio in Lyon, he decided to move to France.

He had become known not only for his skill in preserving the original features of an old house but also in introducing modern architectural idioms, using contemporary materials, without disturbing the balance and harmony of the building. A stone staircase would suddenly continue in a cantilevered glass and polished aluminium flight of steps, or glass panels would be inserted into the brick wall of an early nineteenth-century house in the Loire valley to open up a vista of the river. His work featured regularly in architectural magazines on both sides of the Channel. His clients were mainly wealthy middle-class British expatriates who formed a new wave of immigrants after the State of Emergency had been declared in Britain. Anthony had happily settled in France, and when Mark asked him whether he would come back to Britain, his answer was an unambiguous 'No'.

'Will you stay with James or do you want to come to Cambridge Place? You can sleep in your old bed. You'll find your bedroom practically as you left it. Do you know that since your departure you've never been back, not even for a single night?' If Mark was waiting for an explanation, it was not forthcoming. At the sight of his brother Mark experienced a wave of nostalgia.

Anthony must also remember their bachelor years after their graduation when James and Clarissa decided to move to Belgravia, surrendering the house to them. The first dinner for two they jointly improvised in the pristine kitchen. The dinner parties they gave for friends and colleagues. The flood in the staircase after a downpour caused by a blocked gutter when Mark had climbed out onto the roof in his swimming trunks to remove the muck. A Christmas party when the tree caught fire after Anthony insisted that they should decorate it with real candles instead of electric lights.

Then their paths separated. Mark met Anne. Anthony

remained in the house and soon was joined by his then girl-friend. He stayed there until he decided to emigrate to France.

'I'll stay in Belgravia if you don't mind. I think James might want to have company tonight. I can't imagine his feelings: to be alone after sharing his life with Clarissa for well over half a century.'

In the taxi, Anthony listened intently to Mark without interrupting him even once. Clarissa's death, Fiona Cartwright's unexplained tragedy, Dufresne's visit, the accident and the interview in Paddington Green were too much to grasp. He responded to Mark's story only after the taxi pulled up in front of their grandparents' house. As they walked up the steps to the door, smiling at Mark, Anthony said:

'You know what? You should come with Yasmina to live in France. There are excellent neuroscience centres across the Channel. The Salpêtrière in Paris, I'm sure you know it better than I do, has a worldwide reputation. They probably have everything you need and with your standing in the profession they would welcome you. That would get rid of Dufresne's unwanted attention. Think about it.'

Mark was stunned by his brother's suggestion: he had previously never entertained the idea of living in France, even after the break-up of his marriage. His work had firmly anchored him in London. With Anthony already living abroad he would not have left his grandparents, particularly as Clarissa's illness was becoming progressively incapacitating. James would not have held him back, but Mark had known all along that he would not desert his grandparents.

'The choice of a lifetime,' Anthony added with theatrical flourish.

Mark contemplated his brother's proposal. With Clarissa's death James had regained his independence and he could rely on Agnieta who would look after him on a daily basis. The idea that he and Yasmina could start a new life in France suddenly appeared attractive.

'I'll think about it.' His response slipped out easily, an automatic reaction to bring the conversation to an end. As they mounted the steps he wanted to reassure Anthony that he did not dismiss his suggestion out of hand.

'We can talk about moving to France when we have a little bit more time. Perhaps after the funeral when both Yasmina and Hélène will be with us.'

As James came to greet them, Mark noticed Anthony's barely disguised surprise at their grandfather's sudden deterioration. He attempted to look at him dispassionately, but James had aged years during the last few weeks. While his features had not changed much, it was his posture that had abruptly collapsed as if with Clarissa's death the spring holding up his military bearing had been unwound. He had not developed a stoop but his erect poise had gone. A subtle forward incline of the shoulders. A slight drooping of the chin. To strangers he still appeared to be a well-preserved man in his eighties, but Mark could see that Anthony was shocked by what he saw. He looked at his brother and their eyes met. They did not need to speak: each knew what the other thought. Somehow at that moment their grandmother's death had brought back the intimacy of their childhood.

Spontaneously both men stepped forward to hug their grandfather – something they would never have done normally. Mark instantaneously recognised the faint odour of James's aftershave: he had used the same masculine fragrance since time immemorial or at least since Mark became aware of his grandfather's shaving habits. The room remained silent. The thin afternoon sunshine illuminated the three standing figures in the middle of the room.

Behind James, Agnieta had silently entered. Anthony rushed to her and kissed her.

'I'll prepare a light lunch for you,' she said and withdrew into the kitchen. Still without saying a word, James accompanied Anthony to the bedroom followed by Mark. As he watched his grandfather and brother neither of them spoke, since there was nothing to say.

Over lunch they discussed the arrangements for the next couple of days. Clarissa, according to her wish, was to be cremated. James had strict instructions from her concerning the service. Everything was set: the funeral would take place the next day, six days after Clarissa's death.

21

Mark woke early after a fitful sleep. He could hear the rain drumming on the windowpanes. The room was dark; the dawn had not yet broken. The alarm clock showed five o'clock. Even if he could escape back to unconsciousness it was too late to try to sleep and too early to get out of the bed to have a run in the park. He was toying with the idea of having a shower, and then reading in his study but inertia had overcome him.

With open eyes, he lay motionless on his back, unable to move as if held in a vice. Depression had suddenly descended upon him. He felt paralysed and frightened. This was a feeling he had never encountered before, for depression was something other people had. Of course he knew the warning signs and the symptomatology, and listened to the history of his patients whom he was there to help. An abyss had opened up before him and he was terrified of falling into it. Was this really how they felt?

Next to him, Yasmina had stirred. Still half asleep, she turned towards him and her outstretched arm landed on Mark's shoulder. He drew her close to him and buried his face between her breasts. The warmth of her body comforted him and he felt an urge to make love to her, yet he remained in the same position, moving only gently to hold her in his arms.

When they finally got up, the rain was still falling, insidiously and persistently, soaking the little garden. Dead leaves had blocked the gutter and the pavement was flooded in front of the house.

When they arrived at the Belgravia flat, everybody was waiting for them. Hélène had joined Anthony after she had arrived at St Pancras the night before. Mark embraced her: he silently acknowledged his sister-in-law's elegance. She was wearing a black Chanel suit. At his question she assured him that the children were in safe hands, and anyway she and Anthony were travelling back to Paris after the funeral.

Without any previous notice, Emily, Clarissa's sister, whom Mark had nearly forgotten, turned up from Cornwall. She had been absent from their life throughout the years, and the relationship between the two sisters was rather distant, being restricted to not much more than the annual exchange of Christmas cards. In these Emily usually gave a glowing account of her artistic exploits as a sculptor, which somehow had never reached the pages of the national press.

The personality and temperament of the two sisters might have been different, but Emily bore a striking resemblance to her elder sibling. Looking at her, Mark was reminded of the long-lost beauty of Clarissa. While members of the family were drinking coffee, served by Agnieta with slices of Madeira cake in the dining room, James was pacing up and down in the hall; he was too impatient to sit down.

'Let's go,' he said, although it was only ten o'clock and the service was not going to start until eleven. In better weather they might have walked to Holy Trinity at the bottom of Sloane Street. The church was barely half a mile away but they did not want to dodge the rain under umbrellas and instead called for two taxis. James, Mark and Anthony travelled in the first, and Yasmina, Hélène, Emily and Agnieta squeezed into the second. James had also asked Anne to join them but she had decided to make her own way from Bedford Square: the trial she was conducting was adjourned to allow her to attend the funeral.

The church was empty when they arrived, and only an odd tourist was wandering around seeking shelter from the rain. James with his two grandsons went to see the priest to discuss last-minute details. The Reverend Oliver Easton was a soft-spoken man in his late fifties who over the years had got to know the Chadwicks. The relationship had never deepened into friendship but was warmer than the customary contact between priests and parishioners in central London. Easton was an erudite man with a doctorate of divinity from Durham University. 'Far too clever for the job' was Clarissa's double-edged praise after their first encounter; yet soon she learned to appreciate Easton's acute yet charitable observations about the delicate affairs of his parish and the wider problems of the Anglican Communion.

During Clarissa's illness James had accepted and appreciated his support. Easton's regular visits had become one of the highlights of the week. He was a good companion, since between them they could cover practically any topic from the history of the exploration of fossil fuels to the expulsion of the Huguenots from France. As Clarissa had become more and more withdrawn and communication with her fraught and strenuous, the chats with Easton over a generous measure of Scotch provided a refreshing interlude in James's weekly routine.

By the time the three men returned to the nave, the vergers were standing at the door ready to distribute the Order of Service to the first arrivals. As Mark walked down the nave, the memory of his unscheduled visit to St Mary's on Paddington Green before the interview with Templeton still lingered in his mind. Unaccountably, the serenity of those fleeting moments had vividly survived the tumultuous events of the last few days.

Unlike his grandparents Mark rarely paid visits to this church. Surveying the neo-Gothic interior, he was impressed by the flowing richness of architectural detail: the pulpit with its striking multicoloured marble, the florid statuary, the exquisite organ grille and the marble reredos behind the altar, but above all the enormous east window. With scenes from the Old and New Testaments above the serried ranks of prophets and saints, it dominated the church and Mark's eyes returned again and again to rest on the exuberance of the stained glass. He recalled Clarissa's explanation during his first visit here, at a carol service before Christmas, that this late-nineteenth-century church had been invested with all the creative energy of the Arts and Crafts movement to showcase the design of the age. It was Anthony, going through a phase of infatuation with minimalist architecture, who was less than complimentary about what he had called a bombastic mixture of pre-Raphaelite excess and Italianate overindulgence. Yet today even Anthony had to admit, as he whispered to Mark, that the church, with all the chandeliers lit and candles burning, and the abundant yet restrained arrangements of white flowers, looked at its best. Panels of the painted glass windows threw broken rainbows on the floor.

They did not expect a large attendance. One of the drawbacks of long life is losing one's friends. Mark knew that for James and Clarissa one of the most painful events of the year was to go through their respective address books in preparation for writing their Christmas cards. They had never computerised their list of addresses, despite Mark's pleading that it would make a world of difference, being so much easier to retrieve or edit. Ignoring him, they stubbornly retained their old-fashioned leather-bound address books. This ritual had inadvertently turned into the annual roll call of the deaths of their friends and as they recited name after name, more and more people seemed to have perished during the year and their entry in the address book was cancelled.

'We should cross names out only lightly in pencil,' insisted James as if a slight stroke in graphite would make death less final, with a better chance of resurrection, than the more permanent deletion in ink. At each entry they would remember those who had departed during the year: a procedure painful, but also cathartic; secretly knowing but not admitting that they were preparing for their own deaths. And so, now it was Clarissa's turn.

At half past ten, the pallbearers brought in the coffin and lowered it onto the catafalque in front of the altar. Exactly at eleven o'clock the service began. At the sound of Bach, James, flanked by his two grandsons, walked down the nave, followed by Yasmina, Hélène and Emily. As the family filed into the first row, reserved for them, Mark turned around and in the pew behind him he saw Anne sitting between Daniel and Chris. Further back he spotted Catherine and Maria Perez, Blakemore and Gillian, and some of his students who had volunteered for his experimental study. To his amazement the attendance was much larger than he expected. He felt an unexpected rush of emotion seeing so many of his colleagues: he was moved by their support. He saw members of Yasmina's and Agnieta's family and neighbours from Belgravia, but many people he did not know. They were mainly elderly, and some must have been James's old friends together with members of the congregation his grandparents had encountered during the years.

Turning back to face the altar, he suddenly froze. For a split second he imagined that he had caught in a flash the sight of Dufresne. Surely a mistake, a mirage, an optical illusion, Mark thought, he wouldn't come to Clarissa's funeral: he doesn't have any business being here. But a second glance expelled any lingering doubt: Dufresne, immaculately dressed in a black suit with a white shirt and black tie, was sitting farthest away from him at diagonally the opposite end of the nave, in the last seat of the last pew. For an instant their eyes met. Dufresne slightly bowed his head, as if giving notice: I am here. A surge of revulsion ran through Mark's body while he forced himself to follow the service. They were standing for The Sentences:

'*I am the resurrection and the Life, saith the Lord ...*' but the words of St John became blurred: he was unable to focus. After a hymn, the choir sang Psalm 23: '*The Lord is my shepherd ...*' But he could not hear the music. He could not suppress his rage. Dufresne did not have any right to be here, to pressurise him, to follow him like a hound its prey. It was only when Easton mounted the pulpit and began his eulogy that Mark was finally able to enter the flow of the service.

As they stood for the blessing, Mark suddenly felt Anthony's hand searching for his; a forgotten intimacy of childhood. They looked at each other, both knowing that a chapter in their life had been finally and forever closed. At the sound of *Nunc Dimittis*, James led the way out of the church followed by members of the family. On either side of the door, they had lined up to receive condolences. Agnieta who had accepted to sit in the second pew as part of the family remained behind for a couple of minutes to say her own private prayer for Clarissa. As the mourners slowly departed, the waltz from *Der Rosenkavalier*, Clarissa's unconventional choice from her favourite opera to send the mourners away in high spirits, reverberated in the emptying church.

During the ceremony the rain had stopped; the clouds had slightly thinned out but the sky remained grey and the air was saturated with moisture. The congregation walked, without unfurling their umbrellas, to the reception in Cadogan Hall just around the corner. This venue was Easton's suggestion and it had proved an excellent idea. Being their nearest concert hall, James and Clarissa had attended many concerts under its roof. Clarissa was particularly fond of the building, and a great admirer of its art deco interior.

Crossing the street to Cadogan Hall, Mark received a message on his PC, flagged as urgent. 'Please come to my office tomorrow at 10.00 a.m. in Home Security Headquarters. The reception will be expecting you. Dufresne.' Reading the curt note he felt nausea. Not at the threatening undercurrent of the note, but the brazen audacity of its timing.

'Anything important?' asked Yasmina.

'Yes, look,' and handed over his mini-PC.

'He might have waited a day or two with this message, instead of summoning you on the day after the funeral. What are you going to do?'

'I'm going to see him, of course.'

By the time Mark and Yasmina entered the Culford Room the reception was well under way: most people had already arrived. Formally dressed waiters offered champagne, fruit juice and mineral water from silver trays, and soon afterwards they appeared bearing large platefuls of hot and cold canapés.

As he was making his way to rejoin Yasmina, who had left his side, Mark picked up fragments of sentences from the animated conversations: 'such a moving service'; 'she must have been a formidable woman'; 'the tribute was just the right length'; 'well-chosen readings'; 'what will James do now?'; 'when young she was the life and soul of parties'; 'lucky the rain stopped'; 'how do you get back to Hampstead?'

He was about to help himself to a flute of champagne, the only one remaining on the tray, when at the last second he had to abort his manoeuvre, realising that someone else was aiming for the glass.

'Oh, I'm sorry, please have this one – more is on its way,' he said, looking up at the owner of the hand to whom he had conceded priority. He was a man in his early thirties whom he had not seen before. Although soberly dressed for the occasion, Mark instinctively felt that this guest did not belong here. Even later, when trying to analyse his reservations with Yasmina, he could not say why he had thought that this man was an intruder.

'I insist that this should be yours, you need it more than I do,' said the man politely, but before Mark could answer another waiter appeared carrying a tray freshly laden with drinks.

'It was a very moving service,' the man added, sipping the champagne. Mark scrutinised his well-groomed, expressionless features before deciding on attack.

'Do we know each other?' The man was taken aback by the direct question: he did not expect to be asked and hesitated slightly before answering.

'We probably haven't met before, but I do know of you.' This is nearer to the truth, thought Mark, but the man continued: 'I work with Judge Bennett at the Old Bailey.' Mark intended to ask him in what capacity but considered that that question would have been too inquisitive. The man, as if he had been reading his thoughts, added:

'My name is John Hetherington. I am one of the clerks.' Mark suddenly regretted his original question: the man was obviously one of Anne's colleagues who came along, at her request, to be her escort for the occasion. I am getting paranoid, he chided himself.

'Nice to meet you,' he said with relief and shook Hetherington's hand. He looked for Anne but realised that she had skipped the reception to get back to court to prepare for her impending summing up of the adjourned case. He scanned the throng in the room but Hetherington had already left. Impulsively, he called Anne to ask about her young colleague. She was surprised at the presence of Hetherington at the funeral. Yes, she acknowledged, John Hetherington was working in the Old Bailey as one of the clerks, and he was jolly good at his job, but no, she had not asked him to join her.

'Why would I have invited him? What on earth for? I hardly know him – he is one of the new boys and we don't have anything in common outside work.' My first instinct was right, thought Mark, before rejoining Yasmina. Hetherington's presence would make sense only if he came as Anne's guest. This clearly not being the case, did he come to spy on Anne? Or was he one of Dufresne's emissaries?

By one o'clock the reception was all but over. James with his grandsons walked back to Holy Trinity to begin the last rite of the funeral to accompany Clarissa's coffin on its final journey to Mortlake Crematorium in Richmond, on the south bank of the river. The undertakers had already loaded the coffin in their car and were waiting to start the engine. Reverend Easton who had left the reception earlier joined them outside the church. Both Yasmina and Hélène expressed their wish to join the men but they accepted their polite refusal: James wanted to make this journey only with his grandsons.

The traffic to Richmond was mercifully fast. James insisted on an intimate farewell and a minimal service. A forlorn organist played Schubert's *Ave Maria*. Easton said prayers. A button was pressed: the curtains parted and the coffin slowly slid out of sight. The irreversibility of this final act struck Mark with unexpected force. He watched James who bowed his head; he could not see whether his grandfather was crying. The last notes of the organ music died off as they left the chapel.

The return journey took much longer: the rush hour had already started. Back in the Belgravia flat Yasmina and Hélène were waiting in the drawing room, while Agnieta was preparing sandwiches and tea in the kitchen.

Having finished their sandwiches and scones, they packed their travelling bags while Mark called a taxi. He and Yasmina decided to accompany Anthony and Hélène to St Pancras and then walk back or take a taxi from the station to Regent's Park. During the first couple of minutes of the ride no one spoke. Mark was exhausted; drained emotionally and physically and yet he felt an abrupt surge of relief. The day was nearly over.

He was sorry to see Anthony leaving: Clarissa's funeral had brought them closer, rekindling memories of their childhood. It was Anthony who broke the silence, revisiting the subject he had brought up on the day of his arrival:

'You know, you should seriously consider living in France. You would be able to continue your research without any interference. Your French is good enough to start a new life. Getting a work permit and later citizenship, if you want, shouldn't be a problem. Yasmina wouldn't be lost either: her subject is in demand and we still have a shortage of university lecturers who speak perfect English. France has clamped down her borders towards immigration from African and Asian countries, and even East Europeans find it difficult to settle, but Anglo-Saxons are welcome for the time being.' Hélène nodded approvingly.

His brother and sister-in-law must have given serious thought to the possibility of their moving to France. Mark did not doubt that they would give all their support, should they embark on emigration. Anthony continued: 'I know you don't want to leave James but you could telephone him every day and visit him fortnightly or even every week: train services are excellent.'

For a while Mark remained silent. The idea, which he had

brushed aside on the day of Anthony's arrival, now seemed not only feasible but increasingly attractive. They were both young enough to start a new life in France. Across the Channel his work was highly esteemed and he was not alien to the research environment. During the years he had established regular exchanges with French neuroscientists, and only last year he had been invited to lecture at St Anne Hospital in Paris.

Anthony pressed on regardless: 'By the way, didn't you get a French prize earlier this year?'

'Yes, I did. The Charcot prize.'

At the acceptance ceremony of the much coveted accolade, named after the outstanding figure of nineteenth-century neurology, attended by the cream of the French medical profession, Mark had delivered his lecture in fluent French.

Mark continued: 'To be able to develop my work in France, after a couple of months of adjustment, wouldn't be a problem. For Yasmina the move might prove more difficult, although her research would open the doors of private institutions, if not universities.' The shock of Dufresne's intrusion at the funeral was still acute. To get away from it all and to free himself of the pressure which had been mounting during the last few days seemed momentarily irresistible. The challenge of re-launching his work in France appealed to him. He knew that his brother was waiting for his answer before his return to Paris, but he was not yet prepared to give it. 'You're both very kind. We're going to consider this option very seriously indeed. It's not an easy decision and not the only one we have to make.'

The taxi pulled up in the driveway of the station. As they entered the departure hall the loudspeaker was just announcing that the 7.32 p.m. Eurostar was ready for boarding. The station was busy: a trainload of passengers from Paris had just disembarked. Near the barrier they had passed a couple of policemen with vicious-looking dogs: the animals were baring their teeth, intent on sinking them into the calves of frightened passengers at the slightest release of their tightly controlled leashes.

Anthony and Hélène had to hurry, since without Personal Identity Databases to be scanned instantaneously, they had to queue with foreigners for passport control. Large notices instructed passengers to select the correct channel for departure. They embraced, bidding farewell. Just before they disappeared from sight, Anthony stopped, turned back and waved at them.

As they left the station, Euston Road was busy with evening traffic and the pavement crowded with people. There was no queue for taxis and within five minutes they were on their way. After a tumultuous day Mark and Yasmina were relieved when they reached the calm of Regent's Park.

22

It was a few minutes before eight o'clock when the driver deposited them in front of their house. After the cab pulled away, disappearing into the Outer Circle, Cambridge Place became completely deserted. The evening was still and the trees were motionless; not even the gentlest breeze ruffled the leaves. Around the street lights clouds of insects were cavorting in the undulating waves of a macabre dance choreographed by death at the end of their lives. At the break of dawn none would be alive.

The houses were dark; their neighbours were out. For a second they stood at the kerb: taking possession of their home filled them with anticipation of a quiet evening spent together to unwind after the funeral. The glow of the automatic lights in their house faintly illuminated the drawing and dining rooms: Mark had recently reset the switches to six o'clock to be in harmony with the autumn dusk. They walked the few steps down to the house, and with the keys in his hand, Mark began to unlock the door.

All of a sudden everything changed. After turning the second lock and pushing the door back, he encountered resistance as it bounced back: the security chain had been bolted on the inside. At the same time, the reassuring bip-bip of the alarm system activated by opening the door failed to sound. The peace of the evening was shattered and the prospect of a quiet night evaporated. Upset and annoyed, he looked at Yasmina:

'Someone must have been in the house. Or probably still is. Don't call the police yet. Wait a second.' He rushed up the steps and sprinted towards Albany Street. The door from the street, leading down to the basement was open. He flew down the few steps and saw with horror that the burglars had demolished the lower half of the basement window. For a second he hesitated. The burglars still might be inside. Then he entered the house. He switched the lanterns on in the hall, released the chain and opened the door for Yasmina.

'We've been burgled.' His initial anger dissipated, and his report was matter-of-fact as if describing someone else's misfortune. 'They broke in from Albany Street. Somehow they must have climbed over the wall. Once they got into the basement area, they would have been safe. They could get on with their business undisturbed. And this you aren't going to believe. They must have gained access to the house by removing the four lower iron bars protecting the basement window before destroying it.'

Yasmina shook her head in disbelief. The horizontal iron bars embedded in the masonry had been deemed to be immovable by the expert who had come to appraise the security of the house a couple of years ago.

'What about the alarm?'

'It must have gone off. But as usual, no one bothers and even if the neighbours had been alerted, the intruders could get on unseen with their job in the basement. After twenty minutes the alarm would have stopped anyway. Just for the record, the house must have been open to Albany Street all this time; anybody could have walked in and helped themselves to anything they cared to take.'

Yasmina interrupted, agitated: 'Do you mean that they found the back door keys to Albany Street and let themselves out?'

'Exactly. The keys are still inside in the open door.'

Yasmina, visibly shaken as she stepped over the threshold, was ushered in by Mark who firmly closed the door behind her. Proceeding systematically from room to room they surveyed the damage. The burglars must have spent a long time in the house: the alarm system later confirmed that they had entered at five and left sixty-five minutes later. From the basement they had forced their way into the hall by partly demolishing the door leading to the ground floor and then run amok throughout the house. They had left nothing unturned. They must have been looking for cash, jewellery and a hidden safe. In their quest, they had rummaged through every drawer, cupboard and box, emptying their contents on the floor, sweeping books from the lower shelves of bookcases in search of a safety box; many were scattered around on the floor.

The house was in a mess, yet the intruders had mercifully refrained from wanton vandalism: no graffiti, no paint stripper and no excrement. Their loot was relatively light: a carriage clock from the dining room, a mother of pearl box with Yasmina's jewellery, a pair of Mark's gold cufflinks, a camera with the latest gadgets, Mark's laptop computer, and a few bottles of champagne. They had probably crammed all these into Yasmina's leather case, which had also disappeared.

'It's odd that they took your computer but not mine,' Yasmina remarked. 'Maybe because yours is a more up-to-date model. Did you have anything irreplaceable on it?'

'Not really. The only file of relevance is the latest version of the grant application. But I have a copy at work, as does Catherine.' Mark tried to suppress a disquieting thought: 'Do you think Dufresne is behind the burglary? At any rate, we should report it to the police.'

'Can't we wait until tomorrow?' Yasmina resisted. Reluctantly, Mark telephoned the police. Then he rang the neighbour's bell in the hope of finding out anything more about the burglary, but no one answered. While waiting for the police they changed their clothes, since in their shock they had so far forgotten to remove what they were wearing for the funeral.

The police arrived within an hour: two officers, the senior in his mid-forties, his younger colleague in his twenties, a fresh-faced youth, probably recently commissioned. They were professional and polite, taking notes, photographing the damage and searching for fingerprints.

'With cameras all around the place,' they said, 'the culprits will be caught.' Their computer screen located all the cameras in Albany Street and although there were none directly aiming at the back door of their house, the officers were confident that others placed nearby at the bus stops would yield enough information.

'We'll contact you as soon as there is any progress,' assured the senior officer, handing his card to Mark. 'Don't hesitate to call us if you discover anything relevant to the burglary.'

Although their behaviour was impeccable, they were relieved when the officers departed.

'I'm famished,' said Mark, 'but we should try to clean up the mess as much as we can. First thing tomorrow morning I'll call Neil to repair the window and the basement door to the hall, and report to the insurance company. But before doing anything else, I should phone James to see how he's getting on. It must be terrible for him on the night of the funeral without Clarissa.'

James answered. His voice was calm, having regained the resonance it had lost before the funeral. He was upset at Mark's news of the burglary and invited them to come over for supper.

'Agnieta could prepare a salad. There's cold chicken left from yesterday.'

'It would be great,' said Mark, 'but we have to deal with the mess. We'll see you tomorrow.' He felt a sudden rush of love for James, so intense that he finished the conversation without saying goodbye.

It was nearly midnight by the time they had cleared up the worst of the mess and a semblance of order had returned. After raiding both refrigerators, Yasmina declared triumphantly: 'We have eggs, smoked salmon and overripe Brie. What about salmon and scrambled eggs followed by cheese? Not exactly short of protein and fat but we don't have much choice.'

It was only after their late-night supper that the full weight of the burglary hit them. The intruders had prised open the shell of their private life: they had torn open their letters to read their correspondence, leafed through family documents and scrutinised their bank and credit card statements. Nothing remained untouched. Their house had been violated, its privacy raped and mugged of its harmony.

The events of the last fortnight had already had their cumulative effects on Mark. So much more than just the burglary. Everything was coming together, pointing to one previously quite unforeseen direction and he could not help feeling that there was yet more to come. True, the burglary with its tedious aftermath of police investigation trailing into the coming months was yet another ordeal he had to face. But more than any trial, the realisation that he had to make a choice tormented him. Dufresne had issued an ultimatum. He knew now, in the light of all that had happened before, that he had to make up his mind. By tomorrow morning. The choice was clearly defined. Either compromise his professional principles by collaborating with Dufresne or, by refusing him, face repercussions with far-reaching consequences for his career and personal life. As he was turning off the lights in the drawing room, he could hear Yasmina calling him at the top of her voice from her study.

'Mark, could you come up – I must show you something.' She must have thought that he was not quick enough responding for she repeated with urgency: 'Come on – you must see this.' Expecting her to be in the bedroom already, he was surprised at finding her in her study. The funeral had drained him emotionally and cleaning up the mess had exhausted him physically. He wanted to end the day and was reluctant to climb the steps to Yasmina's study on the top floor. The unusual shrillness of her voice filled him with apprehension. The landing was set in darkness and only the distant lights in Albany Street filtered through the window on the staircase.

'Look!' exclaimed Yasmina, and Mark instantaneously saw it, even before he entered her study, even before she lifted her head and turned the screen towards him. The letters stared straight into his face: JULIA AMES.

23

The name was written large, nearly filling the entire screen. Mark stood in the open door, mesmerised. Yasmina, visibly shaken and uncomprehending, exploded: 'Who is JULIA AMES? How did her name get on my computer?'

'Did you leave your computer on during the day?' He needed time to gather his thoughts.

'No. I checked my e-mails in the morning, and I clearly remember switching it off before we left to go to the funeral.'

'What about a password?'

Yasmina was not listening. 'On the spur of the moment I decided to check my computer. I thought it was odd that the burglars got away with yours, even if they thought that they might have access to information they needed, and left mine behind. And before I could open anything, this name came up. Automatically, without me touching any keys. Do you understand?'

By now Mark was standing behind Yasmina, who was still watching the screen as if waiting for a delayed explanation to appear. For a moment Mark hesitated and then he said firmly: 'Yes.'

Yasmina jumped to her feet. They were standing so close to each other that Mark felt Yasmina's breath on his face. He wanted to embrace her but she stepped back.

'Shall we sit on the sofa?' Mark suggested and, getting hold of Yasmina's hand, he told her all he knew about Julia Ames. Yasmina did not interrupt him once. When Mark had finished, she remained silent. Mark wondered how many of Yasmina's thoughts would remain unspoken. He was growing impatient and while terrified, he wanted to hear her verdict. But nothing was forthcoming.

In the soft lighting of the study, the name on the screen still confronted them. Like a picture illuminated by spotlights at an exhibition. With voice command Yasmina closed down the screen, expelling the uninvited ghost, the intruder who had insinuated herself by stealth to spoil their life at the end of a long day. Without saying a word Yasmina stood up, walked to her desk and switched off the old-fashioned brass table light. When she finally spoke her voice was lifeless:

'How could you? What a rotten thing to do! Spineless and despicable. Even making allowances for your age at the time. And why didn't you tell me about her earlier? I can understand that when we were getting to know each other you didn't want to confess this particular affair which doesn't show you up in the best possible light. But really, from the moment Templeton first mentioned her name, you must have known that even in death she had become a player in our life. Whether we liked it or not. And as such I should have known about her.' That he could not detect any anger in Yasmina's words hurt him more than wild accusations and angry scenes. She was unnaturally calm.

Mark knew that he had to persuade her. 'I was very inexperienced and we were both very young. As it happens, my relationship with Julia was the unhappiest event of my university years. I'm not the heartless cad you might think.' Mark paused, realising that his sentences were barely coherent. 'Looking back at the affair now, my excuse that I didn't know what to do might seem to be more untenable than it would have been fifteen years ago. Julia was more mature. She wanted to keep the baby, but at the age of twenty-one I wasn't prepared to be a father and certainly wasn't ready to marry. With hindsight, I know that I should have given her more support. I couldn't have foreseen the terrible consequences. How could I? At the time I was desperate to forget about her and to get back to my studies. Her memory has now returned to haunt us.'

'Perhaps in her death she is exacting the price for your cowardice. A posthumous revenge,' interjected Yasmina. 'I'm trying hard to understand you. But I can't escape the dreadful thought that I could have been Julia Ames.' She stopped suddenly. Mark looked at her with a mixture of expectation and fear, like the accused waiting for the sentence. The idea that he might lose Yasmina terrified him. He pulled her near him on the sofa and embraced her so tightly that she cried out. He loosened his grip, and with his left hand still holding her, he began to undress her. At first Yasmina resisted but as Mark fumbled to remove her jumper with one hand, she helped him to take off the rest of her clothes. They ended up naked on the large Chinese rug in the middle of the study.

Yasmina commanded the lights to be extinguished but Mark prevented her: he wanted to see her face beneath his. Their love-making was fierce; their senses enhanced by spontaneity; their awareness sharpened by guilt and remorse; their desire fuelled by grief and the fear that they might lose each other. Mark thought that it was more than an affirmation of love. It was their vow to face the future together. Half an hour later, exhausted, they walked naked down the staircase to their bedroom.

After they had showered, in the darkness of the bedroom Mark kissed Yasmina goodnight. Stretching out, he tried to relax and recall the events of the day from the minute they had arrived in Belgravia for the funeral to their lovemaking a few minutes ago. The pictures he evoked broke the barrier of chronology and streamed through haphazardly, like sequences of a film cut and edited in the wrong order. Beside him Yasmina had already fallen asleep and he could hear her even breathing.

He longed for a peaceful night but sleep evaded him. When it finally arrived, it brought a disturbing dream, which had begun as a tranquil intermezzo. He and Yasmina were travelling to Whitstable. At the station they were met by Chris and Daniel. Carefree, they walked together in the breezy sea air. In the harbour he decided to hire a motorboat with Yasmina, despite warnings from their friends that the sea was already rough. On the seashore red flags were fluttering in the vicious wind. They started the engine and set out for the open sea, heading for the French coast. The waving figures of Chris and Daniel became smaller and finally disappeared on the shore. He wanted to escape, to run away from the life he had left behind.

Suddenly gale-force winds whipped up enormous waves. In a desperate few minutes Mark began to lose control of the boat. He struggled helplessly with the tiller as a huge wave approached, swelling above the horizon. With a terrifying scream Yasmina was swept overboard. He jumped into the heaving water after her but he lost her from his sight. The lashing of the wind burnt his face. He couldn't open his eyes. His mouth was filled with water; he couldn't breathe.

He woke, drenched in perspiration just like on the fateful day when he first encountered Dufresne. He got out of bed, had a cold shower and put on his running gear. Outside, the morning was chilly and the sky clear. The park was silent. Mist lingered as the autumn sun rose behind his house. First he started walking at a fast pace and then, quickening the rhythm of his movements, he began to run at a slow, measured pace around the Outer Circle. He was out of practice at jogging and perspiration collected on his forehead, dripping down his temples and his nose. His tongue tasted the saltiness of sweat.

He felt alive and enjoyed the sensation. Drawing deep regular breaths, his heart was pounding in his chest. When he had completed the full circle, returning to his starting point, he did not walk back to his house. Instead, he found a solitary bench on the edge of Cumberland Green, the large open space opposite Cambridge Place. The bench was covered with dew. With his hand he swept the moisture off and sat down. By now the sun was in charge of the morning and he offered his face to it. With his eyes closed, he stayed there motionless. Then he stood up and walked back towards his home.

24

Yasmina was already in the kitchen fully dressed. She was sitting at the breakfast table, with an empty glass of orange juice and a half-finished bowl of cereal in front of her. As Mark entered Yasmina looked up: 'Would you like a cup of coffee?' she asked. Mark nodded.

'This is a surprise,' he said, dropping a kiss on Yasmina's head. 'Breakfast is my job.'

Yasmina's voice was detached and distant: 'I can't help thinking about Julia Ames.'

Remembering their lovemaking, Mark could not hide his disappointment.

'Last night I thought that even if you couldn't accept the way I treated Julia, at least you understood my predicament.'

'You seem to be forgetting that the "predicament" was entirely hers.' She stressed the word predicament with a quick, scathing glance at Mark. 'She had to have an abortion against her conviction, for goodness sake! You might regard the premature termination of pregnancy as an alternative to contraception, but it isn't!' Mark, still standing in the door of the kitchen, tried to interrupt her.

'Don't you think that's a bit unfair?' But Yasmina was unstoppable.

'It may be my "mixed up" Catholic and Muslim upbringing,' she said with venom, 'but I find your behaviour repulsive.' Her voice rose. 'You deserted her at a time when she needed you most. And you didn't even care. You destroyed her youth and her career. She was condemned to a miserable life from which her suicide might have been an escape, while in the meantime you continued your studies, as if nothing had happened, enjoying all the privileges a rich upper middle-class family could afford. It's unbelievable!'

Mark was not prepared for such an outburst and attempted to pacify Yasmina.

'You've changed your mind since last night. I hoped, obviously in vain, that Julia wouldn't stand between us. I take full responsibility for what happened.'

'Don't you think it's a little bit late?' She was shouting now. 'Without being confronted with your past in the police station, you wouldn't have given a single thought to Julia's fate.

'Mark,' she continued, 'there's something else we should talk about. I know you're very keen for us to have children, preferably as soon as possible. I'm beginning to wonder whether your wish has something to do with your feelings of guilt.'

Mark looked at Yasmina incredulously. 'Yasmina, you're wrong. The one and only reason I want children is because I want to become a father. Surely you realise that one of the reasons my marriage to Anne broke down was that she refused to have children.'

'So why do you take it for granted that I'm prepared to become pregnant in a hurry? I'm still young, and first and foremost I'm determined to get on with my work. I want an academic career and to achieve some recognition in my field.' By now Mark was sitting opposite Yasmina, and he extended his hand towards her arm resting on the table, but to avoid his touch she suddenly stood up. What she said next shocked Mark profoundly.

'I've decided that for the time being it is better for us to separate. Maybe not forever but for some time. I need some breathing space. I've lost faith in you and I'm not sure if I'm living with the same man as before. I know that I should stand by you, but I don't think that at present I would be able to give you the support you need.'

Intuitively Mark sensed that it was pointless to argue with Yasmina. The precipice that had suddenly and unexpectedly opened up between them was widening with every sentence. He was devastated. His whole life had fallen apart so quickly. Everything had been going so smoothly until Dufresne's unexpected visit.

'What do you intend to do?'

'I think the practical arrangements should be quite simple. Everything in the house is yours, or to be precise your grandparents. In due course I'll take my personal belongings. For the time being I'll move back to my parents' house before I find a flat of my own. I will keep in touch, of course.'

'Of course,' echoed Mark.

Yasmina stood up. 'Goodbye, Mark.'

He remained silent. When he looked up, Yasmina was no longer there. A few seconds later he heard the door of the house closing behind her.

25

Dufresne's office was on the top floor of the building. The large windows afforded an unbroken panorama of the monotonous office blocks of Albert Embankment across the river. Dufresne was in a jovial mood. They had shaken hands and he waved Mark into the armchair opposite his. After Mark declined coffee, Dufresne, making no allowance for small talk, asked point-blank: 'Have you considered our offer?'

'Yes, I have,' said Mark looking straight into his host's eyes.

'And what's your decision, if I may ask?'

'The answer is no.' If Dufresne was surprised he certainly had an excellent way of disguising it. For a second he seemed to be lost in the study of his fingernails which, Mark could have sworn, had been freshly polished.

'What are you going to do without work? I understand from Blakemore that the Institute doesn't have any future funding for your project.' There would have been if you hadn't interfered, Mark reflected, but instead he stuck to the facts.

'I'll finish the preliminary experiments, and quite possibly we'll have enough data to publish our results in a short paper. And if no further funding is available I'm quite prepared to resign from my job.'

'Don't you think that this is a waste of your talent?'

'Perhaps it is. But this isn't for me to judge. There are other ways and other places I can work.'

'Perhaps you can tell me what are they? Are you going to France? We know that your brother was quite keen for you to join them, although his wife, what is her name ... oh, yes ... Hélène ... her support was less enthusiastic in your absence.'

Dufresne's blatant intrusion into his family affairs still managed to upset Mark. Then the meaning of his dream came back to him.

'It's not your business whether I go to work in France or not. But if you want to know, I've decided to stay in this country.'

'Of course, you can always opt out of our evil system and become a PWI like those gentle people in Whitstable whom you visited in the footsteps of Fiona Cartwright.' By now Mark felt completely at ease.

'You know, Mr Dufresne, that isn't such a bad idea. Is there anything else you wish to discuss? If not, it is better that I take my leave.'

Mark left the room without shaking hands. Dufresne's secretary accompanied him to the lift. From the pain and anguish of the last weeks, he had harvested power and determination. He was at peace with himself. All the ballast of uncertainty and doubt fell away from him. The menace of Dufresne had evaporated. He was free again. He knew exactly what he was going to do. He had made up his mind. He had decided to revisit Whitstable, but first he would complete his experiments.

He walked down the few steps in front of the building and made his way to the nearest underground station.

Acknowledgments

I wish to thank several friends, colleagues and other experts who were generous beyond the call of duty with their time and advice concerning various aspects of this book. My thanks are due to Sir Malcolm Jack, KCB, Former Clerk of the House of Commons for giving advice on constitutional matters; Professor Robert Blackburn, Professor of Constitutional Law, King's College London and Prebendary Reverend Andrew Davis on the Church of England; Professor Emeritus Niall Quinn on clinical manifestations of neurological diseases; Professor Megan Vaughan, Smuts Chair of History of the British Commonwealth, Cambridge University and Dilip Lakhani, Esq. on the fate of the Asian community in East Africa; Dr Patrick Smith, Institute of Psychiatry, King's College London on childhood traumas, Professor Emeritus Charles Polkey on neurosurgery and Nicholas Swan, Esq. on sharing his experience to draw up one of my characters.

I am greatly indebted to Professor Ray Dolland, FRS, for a most useful discussion and for allowing me to 'shadow' one of his colleagues, Dr Tali Sharot. The days I spent in his Institute proved the most enjoyable experience while preparing the manuscript. The experiment on holiday choices is based on Dr Sharot's paradigm, and was published in *Journal of Neuroscience* (29:3760–5, 2009). Of course, thought modification, as described in this book is entirely fictional but it is only a question of time before it becomes a reality.

My special thanks should go to HH Judge Jeremy Connor who not only advised me on legal issues but also made useful comments while reading the manuscript. Elspeth Sinclair gave inestimable help in all aspects in the preparation of the manuscript.

In our fast-shifting political, economic and social world to predict changes even a year ahead is difficult, but to envisage the future a couple of decades hence is impossible. In the past greater writers than the author of this book have proved wrong.